A Heavenly Shade of Blue

Rosie Mitcham

Copyright © 2020 Rosie Mitcham

All rights reserved.

ISBN: 9798571135788

Table of Contents

In the Beginning 4
From His Perspective 18
The Next Step 26
The Morning After 59
A Day Later 94
The Day Trip 108
Alone at Last 119
Time to Forget 137
What Comes Next 146
Time to Heal 161
Next Stop Greenway 168
No Turning Back 180
The Cinderella Moment 192
Dotting the 'I's 198
The Run Up 211
Let it Snow 219
The Hen Party 227
The Biggest Surprise 234
The Big Day 255
Paris in December 265
A Different Corner 275
Making it Happen 286
My Ta-da Moment 298

A Heavenly Shade of Blue

In the Beginning

As I glance out of the window in the general direction of the park, I think that maybe the fresh air might do me good. It is such a beautiful autumnal day that it lifts me and fills me with optimism. There is a definite chill in the air, but the bright sunshine still has a pleasing amount of warmth to it.

I am hoping and praying that today will be a good day. It is exactly three weeks to the day since I took possession of the keys to my lovely new house. Since then, I have painted it from top to bottom in shades of white (possibly fifty) with finishing flourishes courtesy of Farrow & Ball. I have used mostly Stiffkey Blue and Bright White and I have gone to town with the accessories, selecting mainly turquoises and blues teamed with a pretty contrasting pink. If Andrew had moved in as was the original plan, I would have been confronted with griege for breakfast lunch and dinner as what he knew about Interior design you could write on a matchbox.

I think back to my rather self-indulgent shopping trip to Liberty. For me, it was like someone had handed me a golden ticket to Willy Wonka's Chocolate Factory and let me take a swim in a river of chocolate. I never ceased to be amazed by the sheer volume of beautiful curiosities all under one roof I guess they want to give you the feeling of being in an exotic country carefully hunting for that special little gem. Most of which were now safely ensconced in my lovely little house. I practically cleared out their soft furnishings department, so I would say that was a good day, and I often smiled at the memory of it.

I had never been what you would call lucky, cursed probably is a more apt description. But I entered a TV competition on a whim and won an enormous amount of money. What you would describe as a life-changing amount. It had come just at the right time for me as Andrew had left me part way through buying the house, but as I was buying the house outright, it didn't really matter from a financial point of view. It was more the emotional effect it had on me that was the problem. I had started to get panic attacks and dark thoughts when usually I was quite a cheerful person. All part of the grieving process, I suppose. The shock that one day you had your life mapped out in front of you and then the next, nothing. Five years suddenly disappeared down the drain without a trace. I guess he did me a favour in the long run as it meant I had enough money to buy the house outright and enough to purchase a nifty sports car and every woman needs one of those, right?

A cheeky little grey Audi TT which I love far more than I

ever loved him as it has never let me down. I'm a sucker for 80s music so I like to fly around the Surrey countryside with the roof open and the dulcet tones of Wham blasting out. Who doesn't love a bit of Wham? I have to say I was absolutely devastated when George Michael passed away. On Christmas eve I was walking up an escalator in Selfridges with Last Christmas belting out, and the next day we got the sad news that he had died. I cried for a solid three months which was two months and three weeks longer than I had cried about Andrew. I had often dreamed of what life would have been like with George by my side. I envisage us feeding each-other taramasalata with our bare hands and afterwards he would play the piano while I stand next to him and sing, allowing me to take all the credit when really it was all him. He even had two Labradors, and unfortunately a boyfriend. I guess a girl can dream, can't she? I must admit I do love a man that can play the piano I think it means he will be good with his hands. Like an artist or a potter. A man after my own heart who can throw a few shapes or pots.

The two bands I loved from the 80s were Wham and Culture Club mainly for their front men and I still never read the signs. No wonder all my relationships had been doomed from the start. I guess I must have been born without a gaydar unlike my colleague Hazel who reckons hers is set to warp nine. I pause to consider my old boyfriends for a second or the ones that got away as I call them. Slid away is probably more accurate. Makes me shudder to think about it and I wonder what possessed me. My life has changed beyond all recognition and all thanks to Andi Peters and his big wad.

I finish my cup of tea, load the cup in the dishwasher and leave the house. I slowly meander along the street I have grown fond off. Past my favourite Indian restaurant and along the road to the local bakery. I am pretty sure the owner fancies me as he always seems to hold my gaze a bit too long as he hands me my macaroons. I sometimes have to snatch the bag away from him to release his vice like grip on them. That is unless his wife is working and then he practically throws the bag at me and pushes me out of the door. He has already partaken in an extramarital relationship, so rumour has it.

His wife now watches him like a hawk 24/7 in case he is a repeat offender. He has a little van that he uses to do local deliveries to bored housewives mainly. Which is pointless really as most houses are within walking distance of the bakery. It seems he is delivering his cake and eating it.

A lady from the Neighbourhood Watch saw his van parked up for two hours outside one of the big houses. He could have got away with it, but his wife is chairperson of said

Neighbourhood Watch, so she was alerted and sent out to investigate. The lady in questions husband who goes away a lot on business came home and caught them doing the business along with Anton's wife. It was all over the village in no time and is still doing the rounds unlike Anton who has been chained to the cake counter ever since. They say if you want to know what's going on move to a village, so that's what I did.

I think I've watched far too many episodes of Midsomer Murders it has given me a strange perception of what village life is like but, nothing exciting ever seems to happen here I could really do with the distraction.

Anton is now known to everyone as the wife stealer. His wife forgave him but now keeps him on a very short leash. He is an attractive man if you like that sort of thing but not to my taste. All fur coat and no knickers whatever that means, I just wanted to say it, really. With all of Anton's delights laid out before me I decide to treat myself to a lavender cupcake and a box of macaroons. Luckily Anton and his wife are off on a dirty weekend somewhere trying desperately to rekindle their marriage. This is according to Sarah who helps out now and again whilst dishing the dirt on everyone across the counter.

I look at my watch and notice the time is two o'clock.

Good, the park will be empty what with all the children being safely locked up in school. I will sit on a bench with my takeaway tea and my cupcake like the Billy No Mates that I am. I am not having any chocolate today as I have been chocolate free for two hours and two days. It is now all I can think about and I heavily regret going cold turkey on it.

I arrive back at my house and cross the road to the park and sure enough; it is completely empty. I sit on the bench and take a long lingering bite of my macaroon wishing it is the crumbliest, flakiest chocolate in the world and then I see him.

He is walking two Labradors of the Chocolate variety. Somewhere between a dairy milk and a bourbon on the colour wheel. Why couldn't they have been golden retrievers? Talk about rubbing my nose in it. One has a blue collar, and the other the same collar but in red. I imagine taking a big bite out of one of them and laugh inwardly. My chocolate cravings really are getting the better of me. He is dressed in a pair of rather fetching black shorts, Nike trainers and a dark blue Ralph Lauren hoody.

I look up just as he passes by. I can only see him from behind, not that I am complaining as I am sure it must be his best side. Especially in those little shorts of his which hug and caress him in all the right places. His long legs are toned and hairy but not too hairy. He has broad shoulders with nicely toned upper arms probably from lifting weights. He is extremely buff. He has dark hair that seems to fall in perfect waves across the back of his head and is thick and looks perfect to grab hold of in the throes of passion. He is holding an iPhone in one hand and a chocolate bar in the other. He is carefully holding the chocolate bar while he attempts to remove the chocolate with his tongue, all the while exhibiting, what I imagine, is a look of pure pleasure on his face.

Suddenly in that moment I want to be that chocolate bar. I want him to lick every part of me with that strong yet gentle tongue of his. I watch intently as he casually tosses the chocolate wrapper into the bin like it is just another notch on his bedpost. Actually, I wouldn't mind being another notch on his bedpost. I imagine covering myself in chocolate dipping sauce lying back and letting his tongue do the talking.

Barry White is suddenly saying "oh baby" in his deep penetrating voice. I allow it to echo around my head for a while as I dream. I have dark thoughts this time of the chocolate variety, not the depressing thoughts that have been occupying my head. I wouldn't mind taking his whole nut and covering it in chocolate, that is for sure. He is now talking or rather shouting at someone loudly. His voice is deep and buttery. An irresistible cross between Hugh Grant and Rupert Everett. With just the right amount of posh sprinkled in for good measure. What I really want is an audio recording of his voice reading a bedtime story to me. They thought Tom Hardy was sexy on CBeebies, he has nothing on this guy. He produces a slightly chewed tennis ball from his hoody pocket and lobs it all the way across the park. The dogs make chase closely followed by their sexy owner.

For a second I could have sworn he is looking back at me but annoyingly the sun has got in my eyes just at the crucial moment. I watch as the three figures disappear into the trees. Gone, but definitely not forgotten. I retrieve the chocolate wrapper from the bin in which he placed it. I hold it in my hand and gently caress it before placing my hand to my lips. It is the closest I can get to a kiss, but for now it will have to do. I have a very warm feeling as I cross the road to my house that afternoon and I don't think it has anything to do with the unseasonably warm weather we are having.

A couple of days have passed by since our encounter. I consider going back to the park but have decided against it. He probably has more posh girlfriends than he knows what to do with. Real horsey types with big houses and rich parents. I can't compete with them as he is out of my league and I know it. What with my-self having grown up on a council estate and, as they say, you can take the girl out of the council estate, but you can't take the council estate out of the girl. But I am putting that theory to the test.

Now that I have my own money things feel considerably different. I have a reasonable job even if boring sometimes. I work as an admin assistant for a local metal company. We all get on well and help each other get through the working week. I have a house and car that I love, and plenty of money in the bank. He would just be the cherry on the cake. I conclude that things could be worse.

I try not to think of park guy, as I have taken to calling him, over the next few days. My mystery man in his little F… Me shorts. This is code for, I can't think of anything else and he occupies my every waking thought. Even sourdough doesn't do it for me the way it used to. I stare longingly at the chocolate wrapper which I had expertly retrieved from the bin that day. I keep it on the table next to my bed where I hoped he would one day place his phone and iPad before finally drifting off to sleep in my arms. Maybe, perhaps I will buy a few things to prepare for when he inevitably stays the night. It is after all, only a matter of time as he is probably out there somewhere unable to forget about me and desperately trying to find me so he can declare his undying love for me, with any luck.

This weekend I take a trip to a designer outlet for retail therapy. I walk past Ralph Lauren, well his shop anyway. I bet park guy dresses head to toe in Ralph. He probably even has shares in the company as he buys so much of it. I walk in and immediately make my way to the men's section of the shop. I don't have a clue what size I am looking for, but I just know it has to be large judging by those tight-fitting shorts of his and what they were revealing to me. Let's just say, everything had looked to be nicely in proportion from where I was sitting. It suddenly dawns on me I haven't even seen his face yet. I mean, how bad can it be?

Judging by my previous efforts, that was anyone's guess. One boyfriend that I dated for a whole year was purely down to a case of mistaken identity. We worked for the same company but in different departments, and I had never really seen him close up. I'd kept meaning to get my eyes tested but hadn't got around to it. Let's just say when I clapped eyes on him, he wasn't what I was expecting once the blurriness came in to focus. I didn't want to say anything, so I dated him for a year, anyway. He grew on me a bit in that time, but I got contact lenses fairly soon after that. I couldn't afford to make another one of those mistakes.

They say lightning doesn't strike twice, but if he turns out to be terrible in the looks department then I will just walk ten paces behind him and pretend to be a slow walker. I like the back of his head anyway and the way those shorts show off his peachy bottom. I shall loiter around back there and just enjoy the view. Have I mentioned his manly muscular legs that would give Roger Federer a run for his money? I focus on the job in hand and decide on a dark blue robe. I will just leave it casually lying around in my house for him to find.

Aftershave is the next on the hit list. The shop assistant is having a slow morning and takes on the role of personal shopper. She asks me "Who are you buying for?" at which point I pause and ask rather than reply "My boyfriend?"

She steers me towards the Chanel counter. "How about Bleu? Does he have blue eyes?"

The guy could be like cyclops for all I knew and just has one enormous eye in the middle of his forehead. I will spend all my time trying to encourage him to grow a fringe. Who am I kidding? I will be too busy staring at his shorts to be looking into his eyes, anyway. The rest is just window dressing.

I laugh out loud at my own perverted thoughts and realise I am doing this a lot lately. I settle on a bottle of Creed. It's very expensive the shop assistant tells me. I have a Pretty Woman moment and think about asking whether they work on commission but instead buy the biggest one they have as retaliation and a bottle of Bleu just in case he has midnight blue eyes to match. None of my other boyfriends had, so odds on I was due for a blue-eyed boy.

I nearly fall on the floor as she rings it up at the till, but I give the assistant a pained smile and walk out of the shop my bag proudly draped over my arm for all to see. I am feeling much lighter mainly because of the five hundred pounds I have just spent on him. I imagine myself pointing at my bags and casually mouthing to strangers "They are for my boyfriend." Well at least I know he likes blue even if it doesn't match his eyes.

Now what else can I buy for him? In that second, I've just had a nasty thought. What if that hoody isn't his? Maybe it belongs to his blonde haired, blue eyed and probably, long legged girlfriend who is visiting from Scandinavia. She will have lent it to him so she can have the smell of his sweat after he's been out for a run. I feel nauseous. I hate her already. Maybe I will just call it a day before I make a complete tit and arse of myself.

I fear it may already be too late for that. I have already started to put my devious plan into action. I just need to find him and make him fall in love with me. The falling in love I can handle it is the finding him that could be the problem. If only I could find out where he lives. I am working on the Kevin Costner Field of Dreams theory that if you build it, they will come. I hope that one day he will turn up at my door to collect the gifts I have waiting for him. I will just have to wait and see and buy a doorbell with a hidden camera, so I don't miss him when he does.

From His Perspective

As I walk across the park, I become all too aware of someone watching me. Perhaps checking me out even. I am feeling bored and in a mischievous mood, so I decide to get her going a bit. I lift my chocolate bar up to my mouth and lick it seductively, running my tongue around it several times for good measure. I smile to myself as I toss the wrapper into the nearby bin.

Just as I do so a thought suddenly pops into my mind. What if she is about 95 years old and I've just given her a heart attack? I might have to perform CPR until the ambulance arrives. I decide to just act natural and play it cool like Del Boy in Only Fools and Horses. I love that episode I must have seen it about a dozen times at least. Dad loves his old comedies, so we sit down and watch them together sometimes. My inquisitiveness gets the better of me yet again.

I am dying to know what she looks like, so I take my chance and quickly glance behind me. The first thing that catches my eye is her dark hair that hangs in delicate curls across her shoulders closely followed by her huge green eyes that make her look like a beautiful exotic cat. Her full red lips shaped in a perfect cupid's bow and cute little button nose complete the assessment. I decide that I have seen enough; she is absolutely perfect. I wonder where she has been hiding all of my life. She doesn't seem like any of the other girls I have dated. Completely and utterly soulless. They just implore me to shower them with expensive gifts. Not that lack of money is a problem I have to contend with. I'm just bored with empty relationships. I want more, much more. I want the girl on the bench, that I have just watched put a whole cupcake in her mouth all in one go and still looks amazing while she is doing it. She looks as though she is about to leave.

I hide behind a tree without really thinking it through. Maybe I can watch and see where she is going to next. I keep watching and before long she is getting up from her bench and walking in my direction. This cannot be happening to me. I begin to panic. What if she thinks I'm a pervert or something? Hold on a minute, she is taking something out of the bin. It looks like my chocolate wrapper. Maybe she is going to report me for an indecent act with a chocolate bar? She places it carefully in her hand and walks out of the park. I watch as she leaves, crosses the road and places her key in the door of the house opposite. A cute TT is parked on the drive. It suits her. She is certainly a bit of me. I watch her close the door behind her. I am left wondering if she lives alone. She didn't have a ring on her finger I checked that out specifically. I really don't want to get tangled up with a married woman. Although in her case I might make an exception.

I watch as she appears in one of the front bedrooms. She walks over to the window and closes the slats on the blind. I want to know exactly what she is doing up there. I need to know if she is still thinking about me. I doubt it but what I want more than anything is to stand behind her gently lift up her hair and kiss her neck. I will sit down on the bed while she closes the blind and gets ready for me to put a big smile on her face. I do have a habit of getting what I want, and boy do I want her, whatever it takes.

I grab hold of Eric and Ernie and walk back across the road to my house. I feel as though I am so close, I can almost touch her. I can feel a smile spreading across my face. Just the park stands between my bedroom and hers. I wish it didn't. I will try to pluck up the courage to knock on her door tomorrow and introduce myself properly. Maybe.

Damn! I've forgotten to put Nigel away in the garage, and it looks as if it is about to pour down. First world problems, eh? Nigel is my much-loved Ferrari. Carefully selected in the perfect shade of blue. David thinks I bought it because it matches my eyes, even I am not that egotistical! I will put

Nigel away later after I've dropped the dogs back at Mum and Dad's.

I'd lost it with David this afternoon. Was he up to managing Dad's company or not? That was what I wanted to know. My dad had advised me that the best thing to do was to delegate. Why don't you get someone in to manage the business? That way you don't have to bog yourself down with all the trivial stuff. You just sit back and make all the big and important decisions whilst taking home the even bigger bucks. But this, I was finding, is easier said than done. It is in my blood as it was in my dad's blood before me. My dad built the company up from nothing and as a surprise handed it over to me on my 25th birthday. In the last five years, I have taken it to the next level. But that has taken a lot of hard work and dedication.

As a result, my social life and love life are completely non-existent. I am beginning to see Dad's company as a curse rather than a blessing. I can feel myself spiralling into a depression. Something has to change, and fast. David is a good guy, really. He has a lot to cope with at home. Abbey his wife has been diagnosed with ME. That is on top of the fact that his parents disowned him after he married Abbey as they didn't think she was good enough for him. David and I come from very similar backgrounds. Both of us have dads who are self-made men. But whereas my parents are loving and down to earth, his are far too up-themselves to realise how unhappy their son is. My parents know how unhappy I have been; still am possibly.

David turned against the establishment and decided to break free and date a normal girl not of their choosing. He'd grown tired of dating the girls his mother and father deemed suitable for him. He met Abbey and fell in love. He thought his parents would be happy for him. Instead, they cut him off completely leaving him out on his own. He and Abbey married and now have two lovely daughters. They've never met their grandfather or grandmother. It is the grandparent's loss I would say. He doesn't hold any grudges or have a chip on his shoulder or not that I'm aware of. I like to help out when I can. Just to make sure they have everything they need. After all, he's been like my best friend and big brother all rolled into one. Date a normal girl of your choosing that was David's advice. It worked for me. He did have a point there.

I have decided that I desperately want a family. I might only be 30 but I am soon to be 31. I have a strange yearning to become a father and especially want a son. David thinks I love myself so much I will name him after me. Something about that appealed to me. I love my name and don't like to shorten it so maybe Joe could work. Now all I needed was the perfect woman to seal the deal.

I can't help thinking about the stunning girl from the park. She seems to occupy every single one of my thoughts at the moment. Despite this, I still haven't been able to pluck up enough courage to knock on her door. What if she slams the door in my face? I check myself out in the bathroom mirror. Who could resist me? The answer to that is just about everyone I've ever dated so far.

My mobile rings. It is Alan, my godfather, calling to check on how I am doing. Alan is going to supply a quantity of metal to my Engineering company, and he wants to meet up to discuss the finer details with me.

"Can you do lunch?" Alan ask's "How about next week?"

"I can't make lunch," I tell him.

"Can we meet Friday evening after work then?" Alan suggests "I have a work thing happening, why don't you come to that? Friday evening at seven if you are able to make it. I have a nice girl I'd like you to meet and she's just your type. She works in my admin department and she recently split up with her boyfriend. You two might have already met, I think she lives just across the park from you. Long dark curly hair, pretty face and drives an Audi TT. Sound familiar by any chance?"

"Very as it happens. I saw her at the park, and I haven't been able to stop thinking about her since. Is she definitely going to be there?"

"Yes, and I will be sure to give you a special introduction how about that?"

"Then you have yourself a deal and I will see you at seven on Friday".

The Next Step

Finally, the moment has arrived, and I plan to make a late appearance as usual. I wouldn't say it is planned so much as a foregone conclusion. Typically for me, I can't decide what to wear. I have considered pyjamas and a dressing gown but opted for a little black dress and black strappy shoes. Who am I trying to impress, anyway? A few lusty colleagues. I can do without the hassle to be honest.

Robert would fancy me if I turned up in a bin bag and he has told me as much on several occasions in a loud voice across the office. I can't be bothered with the complications of a work romance, anyway. I have been there and worn the t-shirt. It tends to all end badly and one of you then has to leave. Usually, the woman or was the case in my experience. It was just the best way to escape the awkwardness that was left behind.

I have decided to go all out and put-on lacy underwear and suspenders. I may as well give myself a thrill, if no one else. My hair is in an updo with a few curls cascading down the sides. We are supposed to be meeting in a room at the back of the pub. They really have pulled out all the stops. It's a real spit and sawdust affair and no mistake. A cheap buffet and disco to boot are what they have in store for us. Why am I staying sober I ask myself? To save said self from wailing out a rendition of Gloria Gaynor's I Will Survive at the end of the evening, while I cry on Robert's shoulder. It could even end in us having a crafty snog, which we would both bitterly regret come Monday morning. Or even worse, waking up together. Thank god I'm driving, that's all I can say.

Alan, my boss, has mentioned that a friend of his is dropping in and may be looking for a lift home. I hope he's a Wham fan, that's all I can say. Apparently, he doesn't live very far from me, so god only knows who that is. Probably an awful crashing bore from the golf club, I expect. I hate being the last one to get there. I should have thought about that as I was creating a 'floordrobe' in my bedroom. At least it was work colleagues only, no plus ones. I wouldn't have to sit alone rocking in the corner like Norman Bates while everyone is snogging and canoodling with their other half.

I fling open the door full of fake enthusiasm and walk over to a nearby table where I launch my coat onto the back of a chair. As I do so, I can feel someone watching me. It's probably Robert, it usually is. He's a bit miffed that I have been single for a whole six weeks and I'm yet to ask him out. I think I am off men anyway I will stick to the fantasy ones from now on like my park guy. It is much safer that way.

Just for the hell of it I decide to give him a little thrill. It's the only pleasure I get these days since becoming a singleton. Well, that's not strictly true but sex with a chocolate wrapper doesn't count does it? I pretend to drop something on the floor and then accidentally on purpose flash my stockings and suspenders as I do so.

It could be much worse. Like the time Alan came into the admin office to talk to my boss about VAT or something? When, in came muggins here with her skirt tucked in her knickers! I actually got a bonus that year, which was great until I found out I was the only one. Well, if you've got it flaunt it, that's what I say!

I smile to myself, knowing I have done my good dead for the night and made Robert happy. As I gaze across the room, I make eye contact with someone who can only be described as fit as F… I close my mouth, which has started to catch flies. I manage to maintain eye contact with him at all times, in spite of the tingle it was giving me down below.

I recognise her straight away. The hair, the eyes, those lips. She is just as stunning as I remembered if not more so. I just have a few more boxes to tick. Legs, bum and breasts. All present and correct and in perfect order. The suspenders are a pleasing surprise. The only problem is that I now can't unsee them. Not that I want to. In fact, it is all I want to see, right now and much more besides.

The last on the checklist is her voice. What if she has one of those voices that begins to grate after a while? What if she can't pronounce her s's she won't stand a chance with my name? She'd never get her tongue around it, and that would be a pity. I start to hold my breath as she walks over to me. My heart is beating in my chest. I need to get my nerves under control before she notices. She is nodding and smiling at the people stood next to me.

Alan walks over to make an introduction.

"This is Joseph Matthews."

"Nice to meet you, Mr Matthews I'm Jessica Stanning."

Stunning Stanning more like I am now thinking to myself. I bet she hasn't heard that one before.

At least he hasn't made a joke about stunning Stanning, I think to myself. He has passed that test with flying colours. Of course, he would, he's a pro.

I smiled at her formality and everything else that was standing before me.

"You can call me Joseph."

We shook hands. I adopted quite a firm grip. I wanted him to know I wasn't going to be a push-over, but he does look as though he is holding his hand as I withdrew mine, wincing even. I've had him for five minutes and I've broken him already. I hope he will still be able to operate the zip on my dress later. If not, I'd have to do it for him. I'm sure we will work something out.

"Can I get you a drink"? he ask's politely.

"I am fine, thank you". I smile and walk over to the bar.

Hazel brushes past me and whispers in my ear. "He's definitely gay, so don't even bother."

Well, that was like a red rag to a bull. We will see about that; I think to myself as I start to laugh with the barman. He is not really my type, but he would make a very good decoy should the need arise.

Two seconds later, who is beside me, but sexy boots himself.

"I thought you said you didn't want a drink?" he sounds a bit miffed.

"What I meant was I didn't need a man to get it for me." I smile to let him know it is just friendly banter I am not about to give him a hard time. Not unless he wants me to that is.

"So, are you in a relationship"? I ask him. Direct and straight to the point. I've wasted enough time on men to last me a lifetime.

"No, I'm not," he says, "are you?"

"I was, but it didn't work out."

"That's a shame" he says with a large smile on his face that is growing by the second.

I find myself asking him if he likes women, which is a bit of a loaded question.

"Well, I have a very good relationship with my mother if that's what you mean."

He is making this difficult for me not to like him. Why doesn't that surprise me?

"I don't really do relationships," he confesses to me.

There is still hope he just hasn't found the right one, and now he has.

"Why did you and your partner split up,"? he enquires.

"I worry about a lot of things and I'm a bit of a hypochondriac. I think he got fed up with playing my doctor and my fiancé,".

"I wouldn't mind being your doctor," he says.

What he meant was, he wouldn't mind being my gynaecologist, I think to myself. Shit, I wouldn't mind that either, to be honest. I find myself saying "I think I could get undressed in front of you".

He looks taken aback but his retort is "I think I could handle that".

I don't think he has a gay bone in his body. If he has, he is keeping it very well concealed. He is beginning to feel very close to me now. Uncomfortably so. I'm finding it hard to be this near to him and not be able to touch him. I'm not really a touchy-feely person, but if I really fancy someone, my hands develop a mind of their own. It is getting to the stage where every time he looks at me; I get a twitching sensation.

I carefully cross my legs and stare at my diet coke. "Do you live locally"? I ask. Hoping I might bump into him again in the chocolate aisle in Waitrose. As he answers me, I nearly choke on his reply. He's the guy I'm giving a lift home to later. The twitch has now become a thing of the past and had morphed into a dull ache and it is gathering momentum.

"I think I will be taking you home later," I tell him with a smile.

"How can you be so sure?" He asks.

"I live just down the road from you. Alan has asked me to give you a lift home."

"Oh" he says, his cheeks reddening a little.

I don't want to have a When Harry Met Sally moment, so I dull down the conversation a little. We start to chat about this and that, anything and everything, but nothing too heavy. Our gaze never leaving one another, even for a second. It is his voice that is really doing it for me.

At one point in the conversation, I am alternating between his eyes and his lips. I sit watching his mouth opening and closing. He kept moistening his lips every so often and I on the other hand am very moist, thank you very much. I wouldn't mind peeling off his wrapper, putting him in my mouth and experiencing pure joy.

He explains to me how he had taken a trip to Ikea and reorganised his dressing room. Even that, when he spoke about it, was as if he was reading me pages from Fifty Shades of Grey. I was visualising drawer upon drawer of colour coded hand cuffs and blind folds. What is he trying to do to me? I feel certain I could drift off listening to that voice. Allowing it to send me to sleep in its arms. He had the most amazing blue eyes, which I now know so well that they feel like a part of me. I have spent so much time gazing into them. He has the most perfect shaped lips and just the right size. I think his hair is definitely his best feature without a doubt. It seems to stay up all by itself. It appears to support its own weight somehow. It falls in thick dark waves across the back of his head. A neat beard and moustache compliment the look.

As he laughs, I see his teeth for the first time. Not the Hollywood smile I predicted, but good none the less. I have just noticed the small beauty spot on the side of his face. It matches the one I have under my right eye. His arms and shoulders are well built. He probably spends hours pumping weights, building himself up into a sweat. He looks good in his sharp blue suit and white shirt. He seems to have lost his tie and suit jacket, and I hadn't even noticed. I've been far too busy looking at his mouth, I suspect. He has rolled up his shirt sleeves to reveal his toned forearms and what looks like an expensive watch. I wonder if I can locate the heating thermostat. Maybe I could get him down to his underpants. It might be worth a try? I bet he has toned legs underneath those trousers. He tells me that he would like to be able to go for a run every day but doesn't get the time. I wish he would run past my house. I wonder if he owns a pair of shorts like my man in the park. I imagine him covered in sweat after his run. A bead of sweat cascading down his chest and landing on his navel. I could definitely be the one to hold the towel when he gets out of the shower afterwards.

I decide that blue is definitely his colour. His eyes are somewhere between a Hague blue and Stiffkey blue in Farrow & Ball terms. That's how I measure everything these days. We talk about my house renovations and he seems really impressed, or at least he pretends to be. We appear to have the same taste in interior design, which will come in handy when he moves into my place. It turns out we both love Liberty, which surprises me and Dwell which I love equally.

He begins to tell me all about his job in an engineering company. He is playing down what he does, but I think he's just being modest. He probably runs the place as he looks like he has a head for business and hopefully, like Melanie Griffiths in Working Girl, 'a body for sin' with any luck.

He tells me about his watch collection. I wonder how he manages to make everything sound so sexy, even the mundane stuff. Apparently, there is a rare watch that he can't manage to get a hold of. Maybe I will track it down and buy it for him as a gift. What is it with men and watches? I ask myself. I am now sat so close to him that I can smell his aftershave. I ask him what it is? And he tells me to have a guess.

I move in closer and allow my nose and lips to graze his neck. He flinches slightly. I recognise it straight away as Bleu by Chanel.

"I didn't think you'd get that Jess. My mum bought it as a present as she thought the bottle matched my blue eyes. I was hoping for Creed what I wouldn't do for a large bottle of that."

"I will bear that in mind." I make a mental list of things I would like him to do for me in return. It is very extensive.

Blue seems to be a reoccurring theme. It sure is his colour. Blue is my favourite colour too, as it happens. Well, turquoise, which technically is blue and green mixed together. The colour of his eyes and mine combined. I take a glance at my watch and discover we have been talking for two hours now.

"Am I boring you?" He asks.

"I am just aware that I have monopolised you for the last two hours."

He doesn't appear happy. His nostrils are flaring slightly.

"I can go and talk to someone else if you like," he says playfully.

I touch his arm gently and whisper "don't you dare". His eyes are smiling again, and its disaster averted. I notice how sexy he looks when he's angry. I can sense that he is a person that does not take rejection well. Not that he'd have to worry about getting rejected by me; that wasn't going to happen.

I can feel Hazel lurking, and she is not happy. She isn't happy when I talk to Robert, so this must be killing her. Hopefully. As you can tell we don't really get on. We are rivals for Robert's attention, but that might be about to change. Joseph begins to tell me about his family and how he is an only child.

"My mum had real problems conceiving" he confides. "She had lots of miscarriages before she had me. Then when I finally came along, I was like a gift from god I suppose."

I know the feeling; I think to myself. I've been waiting twenty-six long years for you to make an appearance, nearly twenty-seven.

"We're very close Mum and I, I was her little prince when I was growing up."

You're my little prince now, I think to myself in true mob style.

"There is nothing she wouldn't do for me. My dad's great too. We have a lot in common. Well, we both think the world of my mother, anyway."

All this was making him even more tantalising if that was at all possible. I decided there must be a catch somewhere. He just seems too damn perfect to be true. "Do you like animals?"

I ask him. This would be the clincher. I bet he's a cat person and they terrify me. Cats, that is, not cat people. Well, a bit maybe. There was this one time when I was at a friend's house and her cat came and sat down on my lap. Everything was fine while I was stroking the cat, it was purring away quite happily until I tried to get up and then this thing started hissing and dug its claws into me.

"I love dogs" he replies.

Well, I love you; I think to myself.

"My parents have two Labradors, Eric and Ernie. My dad and Grandad used to watch the Christmas specials together when my dad was young. Much in the same way that Dad and I watch repeats of Only Fools and Horses. He still remembers those times with fond memories, as do I."

"The dogs are a lot of fun, plus they help to keep me fit." You don't say, I think to myself.

"Where do you walk them, just out of interest?" I ask.

"The woods mainly," he says.

I wouldn't mind walking in the woods with him, and the dogs can come along too if they like.

"God, I'm hungry" he says suddenly out of nowhere.

The buffet looks less than appetising.

"It's not really my thing," he says, "sausage rolls and stale sandwiches."

"No, nor mine," I agree. "If you could eat anything now, what would it be? Other than me, of course." I tease.

He laughs as I think, please say, me.

"Oh, easy. Big Mac, fries and a strawberry milkshake. No salad on the burger. Or just you." and with that he excuses himself and walks off in the direction of the gents.

I don't have long, so I need to act quickly, I think to myself, as I grab my phone and put in an order to Just Eat. This should earn me extra Brownie points, I hope. At least I could satisfy his hunger if nothing else.

It's 9:45 and Alan is pacing up and down restlessly. He walks over to me just as Joseph returns to the bar. "Can we have our chat now?" he asks.

"Yes, sure" replies Joseph.

He turns to me and says, "Sorry, I'm going to have to love you and leave you." He puts on a sad face and I sigh deeply as I watch him walk away.

Suddenly it dawns on me. Two Labradors hair that falls in

waves. He's the guy from the park. I knew that voice sounded familiar to me. How did the penny not drop sooner? Within a couple of minutes of his leaving, I am feeling completely and utterly bereft. I try to dissect what has just happened. I have already begun to peel back some of his layers. I just hope it won't be like a disappointing game of pass the parcel, and once I have unwrapped everything there will just be something small and meaningless staring back at me. Is he what I want? All I do know is, he is definitely what I need, right now anyway.

Right at that moment, the Just Eat guy arrives with a brown paper bag in his hand. I grab it and clutch it to my chest like my life depends on it or my entire future, anyway.

I walk over to the room where Joseph and Alan are having their little chat. I knock on the glass and they signal for me to enter. I hand Joseph the paper bag.

He looks intrigued. He raises one eyebrow sexily and just as I had the twitch under control; he does the eyebrow thing. I cross my legs, smile, curtsey and announce, "Your dinner has arrived, sir." then close the door behind me.

He opens the bag, looks inside and seems to be suitably impressed. "Thank you" he mouths out to me.

I even remembered the no salad, that should make him

happy. He eyes me through the glass as I blow him a cheeky kiss and coolly walk away. I can feel his eyes following me. He is desperately trying to see where I have disappeared to, but I am out of his eyeline chatting to work colleagues, mainly about him. Or rather I am being pumped for information by everyone except Hazel who is trying to look nonplussed and pretending to examine a broken nail. They are demanding to know what we were talking about for nearly three hours.

Hazel breezes over. "I bet you bored the pants off him, holding him hostage for all that time."

"Not yet," I say, "but I am remaining pleasantly optimistic."

She scowls and walks away "As if that is going to happen" she mutters under her breath.

"I heard that," I say as she walks off.

"You were supposed to," she hisses.

I poke my tongue out at the back of her head. I realise he is still watching me through the glass. Damn. I wanted him to think I'm a nice girl or at least until I get him where I want him then he will realise that naughty is a more apt description.

But he is highly amused at the floor show that is going on. Two women having a cat fight over him, he's in his element.

Typical man. He'll have us down to our undies mud wrestling on the floor next. Winner takes all. Hazel and I, that is.

He is beckoning me over to him. Alan is back with his wife again doing the rounds making polite conversation.

"Come and sit with me," he pleads "I'm all alone." He flutters his long eyelashes at me. "You bought me dinner, the least you can do is sit and watch me eat it."

"Thanks," I say, "you're so thoughtful."

I wonder if he sucks his chips the same way as his chocolate. He playfully pretends to feed me, then just as the chip reaches my mouth, he pulls it away again. I frown at him, so next time he puts the chip in my mouth. I pick one up and feed it to him. "Here comes the aeroplane."

"We didn't have that in my house."

"Sorry" I say, "Was it, here comes the private jet or here comes the Orient Express?"

"No, Mum used to make up stories about me not being able to climb up the magic beanstalk if I didn't eat my food. Anyway, are you making fun of the way I speak?" he says sounding hurt.

"No, I love the way you speak, your voice does things to me."

"What kind of things?"

"It makes me go weak at the knees if you must know."

"That reminds me" I tell him "I knew we'd met before. I saw you at the park a couple of weeks ago."

He looks guilty. "I wasn't going to say anything about that" he says, looking shifty.

"I've spent the last two weeks thinking about you."

"Have you?" he says in mock innocence.

"You and that damn chocolate bar. The way you licked off the chocolate with your tongue. The way you rolled your tongue around it. I wanted that to be me!"

"Well, you only had to ask. I could quite happily cover you in chocolate and lick it off any time you want" he says, his voice sounding even more buttery and his smile even bigger than ever.

We spend the next few minutes just eyeing each other intently.

"I've not been lucky in love," he tells me.

"Me neither," I reply. "I just want to be with someone who takes me to that special place."

"What do you mean?" he asks.

"I feel as if I've been sold a ticket for a place that doesn't exist. I'm fed up with wet weekends in horrible places. I want my trip to paradise. Where the sun always shines on white sandy beaches and beautiful bearded men in little black shorts fan my naked body with palm leaves. I want my happily ever after."

"That's what we all want," he says in agreement "but there are no guarantees. Eight weeks is the longest relationship I've ever had. And to be honest, I only saw her about half a dozen times. The sex was lacklustre, to say the least. It all ended really badly with her full of bitterness and resentment. The problem is, I'm a workaholic which means I don't have the time to put the effort in at home as well. She wanted all my attention, and I couldn't give it to her. So, she got fed up and left. How would you deal with me not being around that much?"

I feel as though I have just been asked the million-pound question on Who Wants to be a Millionaire? I would have to think on my feet. "I would devise a traffic light system. It would start with green. That would be a text to ask: when are you coming home? After which I would allow a suitable amount of time before sending the amber text which would read I.R.T.F.U.N."

"Dare I ask what that stands for?" he says, looking quizzical.

"I'm Ready To F... you Now!"

"What is the red one for?" he asks.

"Too late, I've started without you!"

"Maybe I would let you pick out what you wanted me to be wearing when you got home before you went to work. That way, it would be fresh in your mind. Make you work that little quicker. Just call it time management."

"Good idea" he says, looking suitably shell shocked.

I smile to myself as I can see he is completely lost for words. I am really enjoying this game of cat and mouse we are having.

"I just want to have what my mum and dad have. Theirs is a real love story. My mum married beneath her. Despite which, my dad has gone on to make a good life for them both. They both love each other so much. That's what I want in life."

Let me give it to you, I think to myself. I want to.

"I want you to convince me that you love me. Act if you need to and make me believe it."

Where is this coming from? I don't know if I am auditioning for a boyfriend or a part in Phantom of the Opera, we've only known each other for three and a half hours. Well, technically, two weeks, three hours and thirty minutes. I can feel myself beginning to sweat. How difficult could this be? A gorgeous man is begging me to kiss him. I lean into him and place my lips on his. I start gently and slowly before increasing the pressure. I stroke his face. The combination of his full lips and soft bristly facial hair is making me smile. I sense he is taking this all very seriously, so I stop smiling, pull myself together and concentrate.

By this time, I am actually pretty much eating him alive, but he doesn't seem to mind. My hand wanders into his shirt a couple of times and caresses his muscular chest. He isn't the only one who can do two things at once. I end with a succession of open-mouthed kisses as a finale. I am feeling quite breathless by now, as I reluctantly pull my mouth away from his.

I mutter in my most seductive voice "God I love you" and to my surprise he whispers in my ear.

"I love you too" as he plants several kisses on the side of my neck.

It was as if he had suddenly realised his mistake. He looks

a bit flustered. I turn away momentarily and then turn back to see him reprimanding himself. He is hitting his forehead with the palm of his hand. We are only supposed to be acting after all, although my acting had been minimal, more of a cameo role. Alan has reappeared at the door.

"If you still want a lift home, I'll be leaving at eleven if you want me to take you to paradise?" I laugh out loud, realising how filthy that sounded. "You know, the happy ending I promised you. The happily ever after I mean."

He now looks completely confused. I feel quite sorry for him. He might be four years my senior but compared to me he was a novice at this. He is toast, and he knows it. I feel like Mrs Robinson in the graduate except he is supposed to be teaching me not the other way around. I feel like Yoda to his Obi Wan Kenobi. The thought of his light sabre was all that had kept me going for the last two weeks. I just hope it is up to the job, but only time will tell.

The karaoke machine has just become free. I run over and start to belt out "Believe" by Cher. Somewhat of a mantra for me. It had helped me through all of my failed relationships. As I look across, he is watching me now open-mouthed. He really had no idea what he is getting himself into. He didn't know I could sing. How would he? I was full of surprises he would soon learn that about me. It is 10:55 and I just have time to belt out a Wham classic "I'm Your Man". One of my personal favourites but as they are all my favourites, it is like choosing your favourite child.

The room had begun to dwindle; I hope it isn't down to me. Although, it wouldn't be the first time I had cleared a room. There are just a few of us hardcore ones left now. Hazel is loitering beside me and moves in for a big hug. I am gob smacked until I realised, she is using me as a prop to hold her up. The buffet food had been so awful that everyone had taken to the drink and is now pissed out of their tiny minds. Except me, of course, who needs her mind to be fresh as a daisy for when I make my move.

Someone, Hazel's delegated driver I presume, has wandered over to me and released me from her vice like grip. I watch them dawdle to the car and then there she goes. Her head bowed as she releases the alcohol from her system onto the ground in the carpark. Her driver promptly jumping into the driver's seat and leaving her to it.

Now that's why I didn't drink, I think to myself as I put on my coat and saunter reluctantly to the car. It had been a brilliant night, after all. They say that when you are not looking forward to something, that's when you can have the best night of your life. This one was certainly up there with those. It is now 11:03 as I start the engine and drive slowly to the entrance. That was it, I guess, or so I thought.

The next thing I hear is a sudden banging on the window. I scream loudly and mouth out something rude that begins with F. I look up to see his face pressed up against it. "You frightened the crap out of me. I thought you might have an axe in your hand. Turns out you were just pleased to see me."

He laughs and makes an apology. "I didn't want you to drive off without me, that's all." He runs around to the passenger side and jumps in. He turns to look at me and says naughtily "Now you've got me here, what are you going to do with me?"

"That is for me to know and you to find out," I tease.

He raises his eyebrows. I fiddle with the car radio and settle on Treasure by Bruno Mars. I then show all my best dance moves. Jiggling about in the seat as I drive. We reach a set of traffic lights and I decide to go for it. Like you do when no-one is around. Dance like nobody's watching, that's what they say. Except he is doing exactly that and gives me a sideways look.

"I am still here, you know, or had you forgotten?" I had, actually.

"I'm sorry I love Bruno Mars, so shoot me."

"That won't be necessary. Besides, I have a little dance around to Bruno Mars in the kitchen sometimes. Bust a few moves while I wait for the microwave to ping."

"What do you wear while you're busting these moves," I ask cheekily.

"Nothing" he says smiling naughtily again.

Thank you for that, I think to myself. That will keep me going when I am lying in bed tonight alone. I fall silent and allow my imagination to go into overdrive.

As we get closer, he asks "Do you mind if we make a slight detour?"

My mind goes from 0 to 60 in 6 seconds. "Where to?" I ask.

"I thought we could go to your place, if that's ok. I'd like to stay over."

You can make it the rest of your life if you like is what I wanted to say but resisted the temptation. I'm so glad I decided to tidy up before I left. Although I'm sure l left his discarded chocolate wrapper next to the bed where it has lain for the last two weeks. I like to just stroke it from time to time, like some weird chocolate lady. I'd have to create a diversion somehow. I'm sure I'll think of something.

"You don't have any overnight things". I say to him.

He points at his gym bag.

"Were you not intending to go home tonight?" I ask.

"Let's just say, I had a feeling I might need it."

I'm beginning to think he has engineered the whole thing. How could he? He didn't know I was going to be there. Maybe he is a womaniser after all? I ponder for a second, which was long enough to decide that I do hope so. I need a man who knows exactly what he's doing, allowing me to just lie back and enjoy it. We pull into the gravel drive outside my house.

He waits silently as I fiddle with the keys and open the door. I hope he doesn't notice my hands shaking as I try to get the key in the lock. You've got one of those camera doorbells. I've often wondered what I would look like in one of these.

Me too. I think to myself. After all that is why I bought it.

He immediately says to me, "Do you mind if I take a shower?"

Was that a trick question? Feeling as though all my Christmas's, and birthdays had come at once I answer casually. "Of course, I don't mind, but only if I can watch?" I quickly add "I'm joking" which of course I'm not. "Go ahead."

With his gym bag in his hand, he sprints up the stairs.

I was left wondering whether I should follow. Maybe this was just a platonic sleepover. Perhaps his shower was on the blink. Maybe he will slip on his favourite onesie and fall asleep. I am not about to let that happen.

I lock the front door and go upstairs only to find him trying to dry himself with a miniature towel from his gym bag, which didn't cover anything. I throw a towel at him which he expertly catches whilst dropping his towel in the process which I was extremely disappointed about. I point to the Ralph Lauren bath robe I had proudly displayed for all to see.

"You're my first overnight guest." I explain. "You're welcome to use the bathrobe it looks like it's about your size."

Still trying to get the image of his manhood out of my mind, but not too much as that may take a little longer to erase.

"You even have my favourite aftershave" he says surprised.

"Now what are the chances?" I say, trying to sound taken aback.

I watch his hand hover over the Bleu and then he spots the

Creed before saying, "It's huge. I can't believe how big it is!"

"Me neither" I say as I smile at him innocently.

"I've got one of these bathrobes back at home, but in white. I prefer the blue."

"It does look good on you." Even better than I'd hoped. He helps himself to a few sprays of aftershave before asking if I have a spare toothbrush anywhere? I take one out of the drawer, still in its packaging. He'll be wanting me to place a mint on his pillow next. They say woman are high maintenance. I beg to differ.

I am still all of a dither as he walks towards me. I feel as though I have just looked at a shinning, bright lightbulb and I can still see it in front of my eyes except it's not a lightbulb that has been burnt onto my retinas. It gives a new meaning to the phrase lightbulb moment, that is for sure. He gently pushes himself against me and kisses me very hard on the lips. He leaves me in no doubt that this is not the platonic sleepover I feared it might be.

"Come and join me when you're ready" his buttery voice, now practically molten, along with the lower part of my body, which is poised to erupt. Ready, I've been ready for two weeks. So much so, that I'd had to start without him on several occasions.

My heart is racing. Knowing my luck, I will have another panic attack and get carted off in an ambulance. The last thing I see will be him and his appendage waving me goodbye while I sob at what might have been. I take a few deep breaths and I do as I am told. The trouble is, in my mind he has already been catapulted to godlike status. Surely, it can only go downhill from here.

I take a shower, clean my teeth and douse myself in Chanel. I feel as though I am having one of those out of body experiences people talk about. I fasten the clasp on my black lacy bra. My hands start to shake as I put my stockings and suspenders back on. He looks like he is the sort of man that will appreciate it. I pause for a second. I hope I don't go charging in there only to find him curled up in a pair of fleecy pyjamas. I peer around the door like a secret agent. He is holding the chocolate wrapper I had retrieved from the bin. I hope he doesn't have a DNA kit in that gym bag of his.

"I got hungry earlier, I forgot to put it in the bin" I say, lying my arse off. He is examining it, like it is a piece of forensic evidence.

"Do you eat many protein bars?"

What? That can't be right. He is lying there grinning at me.

"You're messing with me, aren't you? It's a chocolate bar," I say, full of embarrassment. He's grinning from ear to ear now. "You saw me take it out of the bin, didn't you?" I ask him. He must have eyes in the back of his head, literally.

"Yep" he replies.

"Well, while we are getting things out in the open, I saw you hiding behind that tree." I say triumphantly. "I wondered what you were doing?"

"Did you think I was a pervert or something?" he says, looking worried.

"No" I say. "I didn't think, so much as hoped." He is smiling broadly now.

"Shut up and come here," he says to me.

As I stand in front of him and my lower half is revealed, his mouth falls open. I have just had the realisation that in my haste to get back to him I have forgotten to put my knickers back on. So, with eyes wide as saucers, he is viewing everything a bit sooner than he anticipated.

"Bloody hell, you don't hang around, do you?"

I say, "Foreplay is just for wimps." Trying to cover up my mistake.

I reach for my dressing gown. It is his time to turn to me and whisper "Don't you dare" as he takes hold of my wrist and gently pulls me down onto the bed. I soon get to experience how that chocolate bar felt as his expert tongue brings the evening to a dramatic conclusion, not once, but twice. He confesses to me he has never done that to a woman before. I'm not sure I believe him. Mind you, it has been a while, and the anticipation of this moment had been with me for some time.

It was now time for me to return the favour. I took him into my mouth as far as he would go. Far enough to get the benefit of the full length of him. With some people it's a whole doughnut they can fit in their mouths. What can I say? He gasped as he came again and again. He had the best sex face I had ever seen. Without a hair out of place, he strode towards the bathroom. Apparently, what I did for him had been a first too. He was 30, for goodness sake. Where had he been? Under a rock. I looked as though someone had pulled me through a hedge backwards. I wouldn't mind being pulled through his hedge backwards, that was for sure.

We swapped places as I went to the bathroom to freshen up. I played with the red blotches on my neck that I always get after a wonderful orgasm. He would be very welcome to worship at my alter whenever he pleased. Every day, twice on

Sunday and more if necessary. I was hoping it wouldn't be awkward when I returned. I've never had a one-night stand before, if that's what this was. This was all new to me. I usually liked to make them wait several months before getting to this point, but somehow the urgency had taken control of me.

He flashes me that killer smile as I enter the bedroom.

"Come here beautiful," he says.

We lay together for a while, just basking in post coitus glory. All I needed now was a flake which I would put in my mouth like a celebratory cigar for a job well done.

"I think we got a step closer to our happily ever after," he says.

"Happy ending, don't you mean?" I say smiling up at him. He laughs at my attempt at humour.

"I can feel myself lying on that beach." He confesses. "Turquoise waters lapping at my feet. Drinking milk from a coconut."

"I have to break it to you." I say, "But that wasn't a coconut."

The Morning After

I open one eye tentatively. Would he have got up quietly, got dressed and left? Maybe it was all just a dream. I could have dreamt the whole thing. I glance across to the other side of the bed. It lies empty, and the cover has been smoothed back into place. The pillow is nicely plumped and arranged. It strikes me that men don't leave things like that, do they? Not in my world, anyway. Not unless it is by way of an apology for having shagged and run.

His gym bag is nowhere to be seen. I check on the time and my clock say's it is 8:45. I walk over to the window and contemplate throwing myself out of it. Instead, I open the blind only to see him stood outside in my bathrobe with who can only be his mum and dad judging by the two familiar Labrador dogs that are bouncing around him while he makes a big fuss of them. That's exactly how he makes me feel every time that he looks at me. Beautifully bouncy.

I decide I need to attack the situation head on. I pull on my dressing gown and head out of the house toward them. They break into a smile as they see me approaching. How did they know he was here?

"Before you ask, we have a tracker on his phone. I like to

know where my son is at all times," she answers.

My face must have said it all.

"Oh, I see." I stammer.

"Do you know Joseph? She thinks we're being serious."

I can feel them all laughing at me and I redden with embarrassment.

"Sorry Jess, I woke up early and texted Mum and Dad just to let them know I was not in any trouble. They usually walk the dogs at this time, so I met them for a chat."

"We're Celine and John, by the way. It is so nice to see Joseph with such a big smile on his face. It makes a nice change."

I think to myself. That is nothing you should have seen him last night. She leans into me and whispers.

"He's been a bit down in the dumps lately. John and I have tried to shake it out of him, but it doesn't seem to work. I don't care what you do to him so long as you cheer him up."

I'm not sure what she was giving me permission to do. Maybe she thought if all else fails I could shag it out of him. I was happy to be her secret agent after all, I was the best woman for the job in my opinion. The only woman for the job, I hope! No other candidates need apply. The position is closed.

"I love the lavender in your garden, it's very pretty," coo's Celine. "I've been meaning to plant more in ours."

The lavender has all but died off now and has turned a light silver colour. I should have got around to dead heading it, but I've been too busy thinking about him. I seem to have had my brain stuck in neutral since my trip to the park. It seems Celine and I have a mutual love of all things lavender, and that's not the only love we share.

"I love the macaroons Anton has in his bakery. I can never seem to get hold of any, though. Apparently a very attractive young lady comes in and buys them all up."

I tut and shake my head. "Excuse me a moment," I say and dash inside. I grab a box of lavender macaroons from the stash in the kitchen and a small muslin bag containing dried lavender.

"A present for you Celine, from one lavender admirer to another" I hand her the small bag which has a pretty purple ribbon tied around it and the box of lilac-coloured macaroons.

"So, it is you then? my macaroon nemesis."

"Yes," I say, "I'm afraid so."

"Well, he did tell us how beautiful you are. We thought he was exaggerating. Didn't we, John?"

She had to nudge poor John, who wasn't listening to a word she was saying. It was as if he had heard it all a million times before.

"Yes, he did" said John, shooting a look at Joseph. Joseph on the other hand did not look happy. His nostrils were starting to flare slightly at all this talk of Anton.

"I think someone might be jealous." said Celine nudging me and gesturing towards her son.

"Don't worry, darling." she says, "He is the wife stealer, and you two aren't married yet. So, I think it means you're safe for the time being." Gently patting his arm. Joseph is growling under his breath. This show of jealousy is getting my heart racing.

I have a feeling Celine and I are going to get on like a house-on-fire. She has a really naughty, mischievous side to her, which I really like. We are already quickly becoming part of the same team. Our only mission is to make her son happy whatever the cost. I will just lie back and take one for the team.

They say their goodbyes and disappear with Eric and Ernie across the park. Joseph takes full advantage of me having my back turned and makes a sprint for the front door. I have trouble keeping up with him, but I catch him just as he reaches the foot of the stairs. I grab hold of his ankle and slowly put my hand up inside his robe and allow it to wander. He pretends to reach forward to kiss me before shaking me off and mounting the stairs two at a time.

It's not on. He has an unfair advantage, what with his legs being twice as long as mine and him being fit as F… I would have to call upon all of my feminine charms to win this one. I decide to fake an injury. I make a yelping noise and clutch at my ankle.

He looks genuinely concerned as he makes his way back down the stairs. It isn't long before he is at my side, rubbing my ankle and making gentle soothing noises. I shout "sucker", but his reactions are again too quick for me. He slips past me and is soon grinning at me through the banisters. I remove my dressing gown to reveal new silk underwear, which was a recent purchase. I go on all fours and crawl like a Siamese cat. The silk disappearing with every movement to reveal my pert bottom. My breasts are held high for all to see in the push-up bra I am wearing.

He watches me, in a now trance like state. I feel like the snake in jungle book, telling him to trust in me as his eyes spin around. So engaged is he, that he hasn't noticed I am already reaching the top of the stairs and gathering momentum with every move. Just then he turns and makes a dash for the bathroom, closing the door behind him, and I can hear the sound of running water.

"I'm running us a bath" he shouts, trying to compete with the sound of the water.

"Can I come in?" I ask.

"No, I'm making everything look nice."

I wonder to myself how he is going to make water look nice when he says.

"My equipment, that is!"

I can hear him laughing at himself. As I enter the bathroom, I must hand it to him. He has done a bloody good job. Now I know how to make something look nice, just plant his nob in the middle of it. Come to think of it, I have just had my garden landscaped and there is a flowerbed that is missing a certain something. I'd rather he planted it in me. Right now!

I have a huge smile on my face as I climb into the bath. His erect manhood hovering just above the top of the water. His hand expertly finds me straight away. His hand now combined with the warm water seems to heighten my sense of arousal. He gestures for me to sit astride him by pointing at me and then down towards himself. I don't need asking twice.

"Go on then, if I really have to" I teased, although I don't want to tease him too much just in case, he takes it away again.

I ride him long and hard. He, on the other hand, just sits back against the curve of the roll-top bath, watching me whilst gently caressing my breasts. I lean forward to find his lips. I take the open-mouthed approach, which he seems to approve of wholeheartedly. His climax is more controlled this time, but no less impressive. My body on the other hand was yet to reach a conclusion.

I think this bothered him a little. It doesn't bother me, it just means that he still has more work to do, a bit more manual labour. He gently picks me up, and with one hand, throws down spare towels on the floor. My best towels, I might add, but I don't say anything, just sigh internally. I lie down on the towels and spread my legs apart for him. Within seconds his head is between them, gently licking and sucking at my tender parts. Just the right amount of tongue pressure was required, but not too much. I'm ashamed to say that by the end of it I was whimpering like a wounded animal as he finished me off.

Which was a bit embarrassing, but I think I managed to style it out?

He kept going and going, hoping for a second succession of orgasms as had happened the previous night. Sure enough, they went off like a miniature firework display in my head. I saw every constellation as I lay on the bathroom floor. I could quote the words of Simon Cowell and tell him, "You don't know how good you are". But he does. He knows exactly how good he is. He has a very smug look on his face to prove it.

"Did I do good baby?" he said, taunting me.

My red blotched throat giving the game away somewhat along with the whimpering noises. What must he think? I was a snivelling wreck on the floor of my own bathroom. I had probably just come all over my best towels.

"Yes, you did" I said in mock reassurance. I think I had thanked him as well at one point whilst clasping my hands together in a prayer like manner.

"I love you" he says and gives me that stupid grin of his.

"I love you too" I say, feeling a bit irritated for no reason. It is as if we are competing to see who could give the best performance. Whilst watching the other one as they explode in a fit of desire. He thinks he has won, but I will get my revenge. I could not help but love him when he looks at me the way he is looking at me now. So, I just smiled and quietly thanked god for bringing him to me.

We put on our dressing gowns and wander downstairs. I enter the kitchen to make a start on breakfast. I feel as though he has earnt it this morning. It is quite late now, so breakfast has quickly turned into brunch. On the way to the kitchen, he spies my white piano. A bit of an indulgence as I don't play, but I fully intend on teaching myself one day, courtesy of You Tube. I love to sing so I thought singing and playing the piano, how hard can it be? I have a lot of newfound respect for Elton John, who makes it look so easy. Like he's just fannying around in a pair of enormous glasses. It's like patting your head and rubbing your stomach at the same time, except harder.

"I can play" he says casually.

"You can't?" I say surprised.

"What did you call me? You know, jealousy is a terrible thing."

Flustered, I say "No, I said…" but before I could complete the sentence he laughs.

"I know what you said I was just teasing you."

I smile and think I wish I had said that now. He was just getting me back for teasing him about Anton. I might have known that one would come back to bite me. He gently lifts the lid and plays the intro of one of my favourite songs. 'Another Love' by Tom Odell.

"I love this song," I say to him "What made you play it?"

"It's one of my favourites," he explains.

I try to impress him by telling him how I love the way it builds. It keeps gathering momentum until it reaches a conclusion right at the end.

"It's a bit like you earlier on the bathroom floor," he says.

"No," I say quickly, "There is no wailing in this song or crying come to that. Didn't you hear the man? His tears have been used up."

"So, have yours" he says as he nods his head and carries on playing. If I didn't love him before, I sure as hell love him now. He has certainly put a very big tick in my box, and not for the first time today. He looks the way he does and plays the piano. I was positively swooning in his perfectness.

"Would you consider stripping off?" Only I would really like to recreate a scene from Pretty Woman where Richard Gere makes love to Julia Roberts against the piano. The keys hitting odd notes as they writhe up against it.

"Maybe after breakfast" he says smiling up at me. I make a mental note to ring the Jewellers later. I want to try to get him the watch he has been looking for. Although, eight thousand pounds on a watch for someone I hardly know. It was a bit out there, even for me, and I still don't know if he is worth it. Mind you, I do have the money and I do like buying people nice things for no particular reason other than it makes me happy. It would be worth it just to see the shock on his face. The annoyance that I had succeeded where he had failed. He was quickly becoming the Moriarty to my Sherlock, and I was starting to really fall for him. I didn't want to. But I felt sure that by next week I would be shouting from the rooftops, "You complete me". Or "You complete asshole" if things took a nasty turn. But let's hope for the former. You just never know how things are going to pan out. Not in my world, anyway. Having acquired a shed load of failed relationships under my belt.

"What do you fancy for breakfast?"

My voice is slightly muffled as I have my head in the back of the fridge.

"You" he says, pausing on the piano for a second to wait for my reply.

"You just did. I now need gratification of the sourdough variety." I was dreading he was going to say something hip like "advo's on toast" or something equally ball-aching. I would be getting avocados delivered from Ocado. There's a song in there somewhere. I have everything crossed it will be something normal.

"Beans on toast with crispy bacon on the side," he says, still playing the piano.

"Yes," I shout from the kitchen. "Sorry I was looking for the bacon and I just found it," I lie. "Sourdough ok?" I enquire.

"Yeah great" he says. Damn that piano. It's getting more attention than I am. The way his fingers are caressing the keys is making me jealous. Just to teach it a lesson, I might have a bonfire later and stick it on top.

I make tea and finish cooking breakfast just as he finishes playing. According to men, food and sex are all they need. I believe it totally. On the other hand, I think women's needs are a bit more sophisticated. Sex and sourdough bread. That was all I needed served up with a large portion of him. His large portion, to be exact.

"We could be like the Von Trapp's," I say to him.

"The who?" he laughs.

"As in the sound of music" I say. "I could sing with our children while you play the piano." I smile, I can tell he is digesting what I have just said, and I can see the cogs turning. What if he doesn't want children?

"You want children then?" Joseph say's smiling.

"Yes" I answer, "Do you?" and eagerly await his reply.

"Yes, I do" Joseph say's looking serious.

I was pleased we have got that subject matter out of the way. It would have been pretty heart breaking if he had said no. He presses me on the subject.

"Boy or girl? Or both?"

"I'd like a son first, and then I don't mind after that," I say to him.

"Same here," he says "I'd really like a son. Someone to pass all my vast knowledge on to," On women, no doubt, and art of the female orgasm.

I anticipate his next question and say, "We could call him Joe Junior." I was expecting him to hate the idea.

"Middle name?"

"Francis" I say. He stares at me now.

"Where did that come from?"

"It is my dad's name," I tell him proudly.

"Mine too!" Joseph says, looking surprised. "Well, middle name anyway. What would you call your daughter if you had one?" he presses me.

"Do you have a favourite grandmother? Most people do." I respond.

"She was called Elouise. She died a couple of years ago. My mothers, mother. But it's a bit old-fashioned, isn't it?"

"How about bringing it up to date with Ella say? I like Ella Grace."

"Well," he says, "that's the kid's names sorted out and we haven't even finished breakfast yet. When do you want to get married?"

I try to shock him by saying "Christmas Eve".

"This Christmas Eve?"

"Why not?" I tell him. "You want a son; he could be your Christmas present."

He tries to do the maths in his head.

"Not this Christmas, we've left it too late for this year, but he could be conceived on Christmas Day."

"Are you in secret talks with my mother?" He asks. "She is

absolutely desperate for a grandchild. I see her poking her head into prams and cooing all over people's children. My dad has to drag her away before she has a restraining order slapped on her."

"She then looks at me and says, Joseph darling, you are not getting any younger,",.

"The thing is, I'm not. What if the entire process takes years like it did for them? They were lucky to get one child. I'm nearly thirty-one. I could end up being too old to play football with my own son."

"Rubbish. You've got a few good years left in you yet." I tell him.

"Anyway." He says, changing the subject, "What are your plans for the wedding then?"

How do I make this sound as if I haven't already been planning it in my head since the first moment I laid eyes on him? I pause for effect. "Well, I thought we could get married in St Anne's church. Followed by a marquis in the garden."

"In December? Won't it be a bit cold?" he says, pulling a face and pretending to shiver.

"We will hire lots of those patio heaters and make it really cosy and romantic. Red and white roses and lots of candles and fur everywhere. We could have three entire days of celebration before going on our honeymoon to a tropical paradise. Where we return as white as when we arrived because we haven't left the room, not even to eat. Well, maybe just to eat. Although we could get room service, it would be quicker. If we were making a baby, we would have to put in the hours and really put our backs into it. We can ask Anton to make the wedding cake."

"I knew he would be mixed up in this somewhere," he tells me.

"Three tiers, one lemon drizzle, one orange drizzle and a large butter cream one at the bottom. Unless you would rather have fruit cake? Oh, and a chocolate fountain to remind us of how we met. A nice bit of nostalgia never goes amiss. I want you to wear a dark blue suit and a white shirt. I want to be weak at the knees as I gaze across at you standing next to me. Oh, and a dark blue car if we can find one to drive us away afterwards."

"How about a blue Ferrari?" he says, laughing. "I know someone who has one of those. I'm sure he will let me borrow it if I ask nicely."

I scowl at him and tell him off for not taking our fantasy wedding seriously enough. The plan is formulating in my mind as we speak. Most guys would be freaked out by this, but he seems to be enjoying himself in my world of make-believe. "You forget" I say, "I was an engaged woman until six weeks ago."

"Thanks for reminding me," he says.

"Look, if I could wave a magic wand and make it all go away, I would. Make it that you are the only man I have ever loved. I already do feel like that, in my mind. Isn't that enough?"

"I guess it is," he says, putting his arms around me. "I guess it will have to be," he says, resigning himself to the fact. "That's enough talk of babies and weddings, let's go out somewhere. How about I give you the tour of my humble abode? We could go and enjoy the sunshine in the garden." He suggests.

"Okay, you're on." I say with enthusiasm as I finish tidying up the breakfast things.

It is mid-October, and the weather is unseasonably mild for the time of year. Blue skies and bright sunshine greet us as we walk across the park. I implore him to re-enact the moment when we had first met. This time he would be looking at me and I would get to gaze upon his perfect face, like in one of those weepy films when they remove the bandages for the heroine to lay eyes on him for the first time. I think I would have felt far too intimidated to talk to him if I'd seen him head on. I would not have been able to get any words out. I would have just sat open-mouthed, staring at his beauty. No change there then. I am wearing my new dress I bought on my little shopping excursion. A Ralph Lauren, naturally, which I have teamed up with a hat I am wearing at a slightly jaunty angle. I imagine this to be how Julia Roberts felt when she was asked to help replace all the divots in that scene from Pretty Woman. I seem to refer back to that film quite a lot, then again, it is one of my favourites. I will be telling Joseph that I think he has a lot of special gifts while I fight back the tears as I say goodbye. He does, but I wouldn't want him to get too big-headed, so I will keep those to myself for now.

I wear my hair loose today and let it cascade across my shoulders. He seems a bit apprehensive, stressed even. "What are you worried about?" I ask with concern. "You know I don't care where you live. You can live in a shed for all I care. If it bothers, you that much, you can come and live with me. After all, we did get married and have a pretend baby this morning. I have enough room for both of us; three of us even." I say smiling as I steal a quick kiss from him. Which turns into a long, lingering kiss and makes us both breathless for a few minutes.

We lean against a tree to finish the kiss. I resist bending one leg like you see in the movies. We don't seem able to keep our hands off each other. I guess that is just how it is at the start of a new relationship. Everything is intensified. Although this did seem to be getting very intense very quickly like a square of dark chocolate melting on your tongue.

We emerge from the park to be confronted by what can only be called a 'ruddy great' mansion. Even the lodge house has a triple garage of its own. A blue Ferrari sits outside one of the garages just winking at us, willing us to take it for a spin with it's come to bed eyes.

So, he wasn't kidding me when he said he knew someone with a blue Ferrari. I bet he got them to re-spray it in just the right shade of blue to match his baby blues.

"The massive house at the back isn't mine." he says, as if this new piece of information is supposed to make me feel better. "It belongs to my parents." He rubs one of my hands soothingly with his thumb. "Don't worry" he says, "I will get my butler to fix you drink to steady your nerves."

He realises he has taken it too far, and that this is not the time to poke fun at me.

"Look baby if you really don't like it, we can get it redecorated to your taste. Like that will make everything alright. Can you make it shrink as well? You can have fun with your Farrow & Ball paint colour charts. We can even see if Laurence Lewellyn Bowen is available to do the work?"

"That would be nice, I quite fancy him." I say with a big smile on my face. I have a thing about men with beards funnily enough. He looks at his phone and pretends to scroll through the contact list.

"Sorry he's not available, he's washing his hair," he says. "George Clark might be available through? We just need to confirm dates." he jokes.

"Great" I say to him "I quite fancy him too". He looks a bit unhappy. "Not as much as I fancy you, of course, I add quickly" whilst giving him a reassuring pat on the arm.

"Oh, you have remembered I'm here then," he says, trying to sound put out.

"You are never far from my thoughts, my darling, you know that." I say fluttering my eyes at him.

"We are very quickly turning into his mum and dad." A horror for most people but, he seems quite happy about the prospect. "I didn't want to tell you about the house yet. I wanted you to get to know me first. I wanted to prove to you that I'm not just a pretentious rich boy. I'm hard working like my dad and I'm good at what I do."

"Which is what, exactly? And don't lie to me". I tell him.

"I'm CEO of an engineering company. The one my dad built up from scratch by himself. It was relatively successful when I took it over five years ago, but now it's going from strength to strength thanks to my business acumen and David's hard work, or should that be the other way around? Don't tell him I said that. I want something to hand over to my son one day. Something he can be proud of. This is all for the future, and that's the reason why I'm doing it. If I work hard now, it will pay off later by enabling me to sit back in my latter years and enjoy myself. With you if you'll still want me by then?"

I flash forward in my mind to him with grey hair and think of Richard Gere. Well, I definitely would, I think to myself.

"You've met Mum and Dad; they are easy to get on with. Mum really likes you I can tell."

I thought it was a bit too soon to be talking about growing old together. In a week's time, maybe. So, I just smile and nod my head. He speaks with enormous passion about it all. I admire him a great deal. Maybe he is husband material. Who was I kidding? He definitely is.

"My parents have a walled garden at the back of the house. It's very private and not overlooked at all."

"Except by your parents." I say quickly.

"They won't be here. It's their day to play bridge with the oldies."

So that's what we will be doing. Having sex in his parent's back garden. It beats watering the herbaceous borders, I suppose.

"I could imagine at the end of Gardeners World Monty Don handing out a list of jobs to do in the garden this weekend. Make hay while the sun shines. Have sex in the potting shed. Roger each other senseless at the back of the garden."

"Well, perhaps he should" says Joseph in fits of laughter. "Imagine the ratings." he says as he carries on laughing. I bet Alan Titchmarsh would be up for it with all those rude books he's written. "House or garden?" he says to me.

"I reckon we should get dirty in the garden and then clean up in the house, or is it the other way around?" I say noticing the hosepipe in the corner. I don't need too much persuasion.

We run to the back of the garden, laughing like a couple

of teenagers. He encourages me to sit down on a garden chair. He doesn't waste any time as he lifts up my dress, not even bothering to remove my underwear, just expertly moves it out of the way enough for him to plunge his tongue inside. I gasp as he makes contact with me. He pays great attention to all the bits I want him to. I lovingly stroke his hair as I really don't want him to stop what he's doing any time soon, possibly ever. He gets me to unzip my dress so he can stroke my nipples while he licks me. After a few minutes, I can't take any more. The orgasms come thick and fast. Yet again he carries on as I produce a second round of orgasms, every bit as dramatic as the first.

I am beginning to get my breath back when he pulls me to my feet. I am just wondering to myself if this is where I get pulled through his hedge backwards when he bends me over and mounts me from behind. I thought pottering in the garden filled me with joy. He could fill me with his joy anytime he wanted! He gently eased himself into me again and again, all the while telling me how much he loves me, until he cannot give any more.

We tidy ourselves up and think about heading to the house. Just then I catch sight of Celine. She is making her way towards us with a tray.

"I thought you could do with refreshments" she says, smiling. I could quite happily have dug a big hole and buried myself in it.

"I thought you were at bridge club Mum," says Joseph looking a bit flushed.

"Oh that, there was a last-minute cancellation. Marjorie has put her hip out." Celine explains. "Don't worry, your father is asleep in front of the TV and I can't find my glasses anywhere, so I didn't see a thing."

"How did you know we were here then?"

"Well, I couldn't see everything. Anyway, your secret's safe with me." That's of small consolation, I think to myself. It will be all around the bridge club, I'm sure.

"As I said earlier dear, as long as you're making my boy happy, I don't care what you do, and he looks very happy. Just maybe check there is no one home next time, eh?" As she walks past him, she gently touches his face and says, "I'd do your trousers up if I were you, you'll catch a cold,".

He looks down and rolls his eyes. He looks at me and mouths out "sorry". We wait till she has gone, and then we run across the garden to the lodge house. He opens the door and pretends to carry me over the threshold. We then collapse in a fit of giggles, thinking about what has just happened. "sorry" he says again, "how was I to know?"

It wasn't his fault. It was just an honest mistake.

"She will soon forget about it," he says, trying to reassure me. "She forgets what she's just had for breakfast some days."

I can't say I will forget it anytime soon. It will remain fixed in my memory forever. Or for a good while at least. Today had been the perfect day, and it isn't over yet. Joseph's phone made little beeping noises. He ignores it before finally picking it up reluctantly. The name David is flashing on the screen. Not that I was looking. Well, only to make sure it wasn't a Swedish woman's name.

"I need to get this, sorry" says Joseph as he walks out of the room. He disappears to a room at the back of the house and closes the door behind him. It must be his study, I presume. I have a good nose around the house. It is tastefully decorated. I recognise the paint choices and can place them on the Farrow & Ball colour chart. Everything is spotless and neutral. What was there not to like? I might stamp a bit of personality on it, but the touches needed would only be minimal. The hallway led to a large kitchen and conservatory. On the other side of the hall was a living room at the front and, what must be, his study at the back. I climb the stairs to have a look at the bedrooms.

There are three good-sized bedrooms and three bathrooms all off a central landing. What I presume to be his bedroom is white with touches of blue. Everything is just as I would expect. A large bed with minimalist pieces of furniture. A large dressing room and a bright contemporary bathroom. I make my way back downstairs, running my hand along the handrail as I walk. He is nowhere to be seen. I would have to get used to this if I was to become a permanent fixture around here. I can't say he hasn't given me a head's up as far as that is concerned. Ten minutes pass by and I am still sat by myself. I want to go back home for a bit. I close the front door and head down the drive. The sun is still shining as I walk across the park and out through the other side. I put the key in the door and let myself in.

I have just sat down when the phone rings. I stare at it as it flashes up 'Joseph, my favourite boyfriend'. Cheeky so-and-so. I didn't even know he had my number as I hadn't had a chance to give it to him yet. He must have got hold of my phone somehow. Maybe last night at the bar, I had been pre-occupied with those eyes of his. I answer it.

"Where are you" he says in his dulcet tones. "I'm lonely" I felt flushed. What sort of relationship was this going to be if

I couldn't look at him or talk to him without going to pieces? He definitely knows how to use that buttery voice of his to its full advantage. He makes every word feel as though I'm taking part in an illicit phone call. I'm thoroughly enjoying it, though, I have to say.

"I've only been gone for ten minutes and anyway you were working when I left," I point out to him.

"Ten minutes, it feels a lot longer than that," he says to me.

"I will lock up and come straight back over to you" I tell him. "You won't have to feel lonely anymore." He mentions to me that David and Abbey would like to come over tomorrow as they really want to meet me.

"Do you mind if they bring the kids with them?" He asks tentatively. "They are lovely kids, but they make a lot a noise and mess. Everything ends up covered in sticky finger marks".

"That" I say "Is why we are doing it at your place, mine is far too fresh out of the box for that. Besides, that means you have to do all the clearing up and I only have to assist. Which I know full well won't be the case."

"Fair enough," he says.

Feeling confident that he can cope without me for another ten minutes, I decide to put down the phone and pop into

Anton's picking up treats for tomorrow. I want to make a good impression on David and Abbey if I intend on becoming a permanent fixture. I purchase lots of sparkly cupcakes and basically everything sugar coated, or unicorn clad I can find before making for the Deli to pick up savoury bits and pieces. I have no idea what they eat, so again I buy pretty much one of everything. I decide we will have a unicorn theme as Joseph mentions that one of the girls, Clara I think, missed out on her birthday party as Abbey wasn't feeling very well. I decide we will give her an impromptu one instead. I pop into a couple of the other village shops before heading off.

Laden down with bags, I head back to the Lodge house after a gentle meander through the park. The sun is so beautiful that I am tempted to sit for a while but feel I have probably kept him waiting long enough. It will do Joseph good to know he can't just click his fingers and I come running. But if he happens to suggest a walk in his parent's garden again, I will throw on my trainers and be straight out of the door quick as a flash.

As I approach the house, I can see him stood on the doorstep. My inquisitive mind wonders what he is up to. Maybe he has sent out a search party to come and find me. He spots me and flashes me one of his smiles. He needs to stop doing that my heart really can't take it. I smile back at him. Yet again, floored by the perfectness of him. I feel like the luckiest girl in the world right now as I walk over to him, place the bags down on the floor and smother him with kisses. I have to go on tiptoes as he towers over me in my white plimsoles.

He gently places me against the wall of the house and kisses my neck. All the while his hands are inside the flared skirt of my dress, caressing my silken clad buttocks. I am just getting carried away in the moment when someone appears next to us. I fully expect to see Celine's poor face as I open my eyes. Not twice in one day, surely?

Joseph stops what he is doing long enough to introduce me to David, his second in command of the company. He was getting paperwork from the car as I turned up. I introduce myself before disappearing into the house in a vast state of embarrassment yet again. This seemed to be becoming a regular thing. I leave Joseph to face the music while I eavesdrop on their conversation.

"Bloody hell mate, where have you been hiding her? No wonder I can't get hold of you these days." jokes David "Punching above your weight, aren't you?"

Joseph agrees with him and say's smugly, "I'm not complaining."

"I can see that." says David. "I'm guessing you'll be taking me up on that offer of working from home". Before heading off across the road to his black Range Rover.

I am just grateful his wife and kids weren't in the car. That could have been awkward to say the least as we pass each other the sandwiches tomorrow. It is bad enough that David is here to witness it. Joseph joins me again. He apologies for not mentioning David being there sooner.

"I was enjoying the moment" he says stroking my arm.

"I bet you did it on purpose," I say to him. "I know what you men are like."

"I just wanted to show you off what's wrong with that?"

"I think you showed me off a bit more than you ought to have done, that's all," I say gently. "We were practically having a ménage à trois."

"I think he was suitably envious. He feels like he already knows you, anyway. I haven't stopped banging on about you since that day in the park. In the end, he was threatening to ask you out for me if I didn't do something. Alan came to the rescue, anyway."

He had my attention now. "What exactly did Alan do?" I enquired. He knew he had some explaining to do if he wanted to get out of this one.

"We got chatting, and I told him I'd met someone. I just happened to tell him what you looked like, and he said that it sounded like someone who worked for him. He said you had just moved into a house not far from me. So, we decided to put our heads together and come up with a plan. I was to turn up at the party as agreed and he would introduce me to you. That was the agreement. The rest would be up to me."

"Co-conspirators, eh?" I'm seeing Alan in a whole new light.

"Besides, it had come to the point where David was begging me to work from home just so he wouldn't have to hear about you anymore."

"I do love you" I say, looking deep and meaningfully into his eyes.

"I can't say I blame you" he says in his usual teasing manner. "I'm a bit in love with me myself" he says. Not just a bit, I ponder silently.

"What shall we do tonight?" he asks. "How about a romantic moonlit stroll in my parents' garden?"

"No chance" I say "We don't want you to get frostbite. It might shatter and fall off." We both laugh raucously at the mere thought of it. I cry internally at the prospect. It would be like someone offering me a juicy chip and then taking it away again. Not that anyone would do that?

"Why don't we, snuggle up in front of the fire and watch a movie of your choosing," he says seductively. I agree to that and decide to choose Pretty Woman. "Has it got Vin Diesel in it," he asks optimistically.

"No" I say sounding irritated. "The clue is in the title. It has a pretty woman in it." He decides to talk through the majority of it. Constantly asking stupid questions like who is the man in the big hat? To be fair, I do that a lot too. Especially if someone I know is watching a programme, I'm not interested in. The only bits he enjoys are the car scenes and the sex scenes. It has reached my favourite part of the film where Julia Roberts talks in a quivering voice about his special gifts. This bit always makes me cry but not tonight I am holding it together for the sake of womankind. I have my reputation to think of.

He asks me, "What are my special gifts?"

He is waiting for me to reel off a great long list of all his amazing attributes. Whit, boyish good looks, sparkling personality. Instead, I opt for "causing me embarrassment in front of your friends and family" I nearly said mine is "picking wronguns" but I decide to keep that to myself. Then again, I hadn't done too badly this time. I ask him what my special gifts are? He places his finger on his chin and pretends to consider for a while.

"Hmmm, you know when you stuck my ...."

"Okay, I get it. You don't need to elaborate, thank you very much!"

"What about that special gift I gave you in the garden when you were bent over?" he says, chuckling to himself.

"Basically, you are my special gift, from god I suppose," I tell him.

"That's right. He gave me very strict instructions." He said to me. "Joseph put on your best Saville Row suit and work that woman up into such a state of sexual arousal that she will weep at your feet. I'd say it was mission accomplished, wouldn't you?"

I just look at him and nod in agreement. I couldn't really argue with that. He takes my hand and pulls me down next to him. He has made a bed on the floor in front of the fire and to my surprise, for once we just kiss and embrace as nothing else seems to matter right in that moment. Eventually we both fall asleep. We wake up just as the final embers of the fire are going out. He decides he will carry me up to bed. This could be a disaster; I think to myself. The whole process seems to take a while and by the time he reaches the top of the stairs he is out of breath. "I thought you said you go running every day?"

"I may have exaggerated a bit. I do run when I go to pick up a takeaway"

He enters the bedroom and hurls me in the general direction of the bed. I bounce not once but twice before landing in a heap on the other side. He doesn't seem to notice as he is still hunched over trying to straighten his back. He looks to see where I am and finds me on the floor where I have landed. He puts out his hand and pulls me to my feet. Now exhausted, we wash and get ready for bed. We snuggle into each other like it is the most natural thing in the world and fall asleep.

A Day Later

The next morning, I awaken to find someone licking my face and something else nudging my hand. I open my eyes to see Eric and Ernie bouncing around at the side of the bed. Joseph on the other hand is in the bath playing with his iPad. I can see myself and his iPad would soon be falling out as, yet again, it is getting more attention than me.

"Mum and Dad have gone out this morning, so I offered to have the boys. I thought we could go for a long walk in the woods later."

"Who will look after the dogs?" I ask teasingly.

"Very funny" he says jovially.

I get undressed and join him in the bath, and I start to rub my foot against his leg.

"Not in front of the children" he says to me and covers Eric's eyes with his hands.

We finish our bath and get out. I am just beginning to worry he has gone off me when I feel a hand between my legs. He teases my breasts while kissing the back of my neck. I can feel his warm breath on me, and it sends a shiver down my spine. Just then I have a terrible thought. What if I turn around to see his dad standing behind me? No. I would know that perfect finger placement anywhere. I turn around to check.

I am greeted by his grinning face, his eyes wide with anticipation. He opts to sit me gently on the side of the bed rather than throwing me this time and slowly enters me. I wrap my legs around his tightly and I thrust in time with him. To my surprise, we both quickly climax in unison for the first time. With him spread out before me, how could I do anything but?

"That's save us a couple of hours," he jokes.

"You must need more practice, if it takes that long" I say and shoot him a look. He smiles and leaves me to get ready.

When I get down-stairs he has made breakfast or at least nipped out to buy it. I notice the Costa wrappers on the counter-top behind him. I decide it is the thought that counts. He has put it on a nice plate and made tea. I accuse him of spoiling me, but he tells me he wants to.

"I feel happier than I have in a long time, maybe ever." He confesses to me.

"Me too," I say as I tuck into my breakfast. "Who wouldn't be happy, this is a good panini."

He laughs. "I'm deadly serious" he says.

"So am I!" Who needs sourdough when I've got him?

We load the dogs into the back of his Porsche Macan. I can't believe this is just his run-around car. Mind you, as they say, his other car is a Ferrari. A blue one called Nigel. He's not sure why it it's called Nigel just that it looked like a Nigel. We hold hands and walk while the dogs run about the woods.

They enjoy themselves chasing squirrels and anything else that moves. It is still early, so we have the woods to ourselves. Just the faint rustle of leaves and the occasional bird song to contend with. A deer bursts into view from the under-growth and then quickly disappears again. I am frightened we are going to have Fenton moment on our hands for a second, but the boys don't seem to notice. Eric is having a contented pee and Ernie is trying to stick his head down a rabbit hole.

I revelled in this bliss filled moment. I feel as though someone has just shoved a Lindt chocolate ball in my mouth and let it melt on my tongue. It occurs to me that maybe I don't need a man, I just need chocolate. I look across at him and decide that maybe I need both. He was proof of that. We chat about anything and everything. I start to think about the surprise I have in store for him later. It was a doozie. Let's just say, I had bought him something new to wear. Not Ralph this time, but something a bit more fetching. It wasn't the watch he yearned for either, not yet anyway. As we reach the final leg of our walk, I start to cry. I can feel myself tearing up and he is wearing his concerned face.

"What's wrong" he asks me.

"Nothing, absolutely nothing," I say. "These are happy tears," I tell him.

"We're like Siamese twins, aren't we?"

"Not really," I say,

"Two sides of the same coin?" He tries.

"Better" I say and offer an alternative, "Celine and John?"

"Definitely," he says in agreement.

We jump in the car and head back to the house. He looks at me and ponders. "What do you want to do tomorrow"

"How do you mean," I ask "aren't you working? Mr workaholic".

"No, not this week. I've taken time off especially," he says proudly. "I want to spend every waking moment with the woman I love."

"But aren't you forgetting something? I work too, you know." I say indignantly.

"But not this week according to Alan." He says pleased with himself.

"So, we get to spend the whole week together, like in Pretty Woman?"

"Are you going to bounce on the bed and sing prince in the bath?"

"I do that already" I tell him. "Bounce off the bed, anyway." He is reminded of last night and looks mortified at the memory of it.

"Sorry about that."

"How's your back," I ask.

"Fine," he says, "Thanks for asking. Fancy a trip to London tomorrow? We could get lunch, have a look around Liberty being as we both like it so much."

"Sounds like a plan" I say enthusiastically. We decide to skip lunch and get on with our preparations for the party. I can't wait to see his face when he collects his surprise. I just hope he doesn't cancel our trip to London off the back of it.

As soon as we get back to the house, I throw myself into the party preparations. Joseph thinks it's a great idea and, of course, he would love to help me. Which actually means in men's talk, sitting and playing on his phone while I do all the donkey work. But I don't mind. To be honest, I was thoroughly enjoying myself. What with me being the big kid that I was and being partial to a unicorn.

I set up a separate table for the two girls. Full of everything money could buy that might be covered in sugar. I really want these people to like me being as Joseph is so fond of them. I will try my best to not make the children sick. I would have to put a limit on the cupcakes and macaroons. Maybe I could set up a ticket system so I could keep a tab on how much sugar they are consuming. I decide to put lots of healthy stuff out for them as well, but what were the chances of them eating that. I sprinkled their table in little sparkly bits and sat the two unicorns in their seats, ready.

The adult table was full of yummy bits from the deli. Sun-dried tomatoes, Humous and pitta breads, couscous, stuffed olives, you name it, I'd bought it. I'd been tempted to bring my chocolate fountain across from the house, but I wasn't sure the bright white walls could handle it. I might have been tempted to dip him into it after they'd gone. Joseph had said I could redecorate, but I don't think that was what he had in mind. I just have time to give Joseph his surprise before the guests are due to arrive. I take his hand and lead him up to the bedroom. "I quickly say, it's not what you think" and I announce a 'ta-da' moment.

The first words out of his mouth are "What the F…!"

Not quite the reaction I was looking for, but we could run with it. "Tonight, for one night only, you are JoJo the magic unicorn." I fall to my knees, clutching my stomach, I am laughing so much. I am thankful that my pelvic floor is still in top form.

"Only for you," he says.

"Think of the children. Their ickle faces."

"They are not my children," he says, getting a bit hot under the collar.

I point out to him. "If Joe junior wants his daddy to dress up as magic unicorn, you'd do it wouldn't you?" I ask, knowing full well that he would. This would be my test to find out if he is good parent material or not.

"What would you like me to do then?" He asks' looking thoroughly fed up.

"Basically, you need to get dressed up and wait outside till we give the signal for you to make your grand entrance".

"Outside, where exactly? I don't want to be seen by every Tom, Dick or Harry who happens to drive past. I'll never live it down."

"I'll tell you what, I will stand next to you mooning so no-one notices you, if it makes you feel better. All your family and friends have seen it, so what's a few more people. Even Alan has seen it." I make a mental note must stop exposing myself!

"Okay," he says "but I want something in return"

"Okay, I can give your horn a stroke later if you like" I laugh at my double entendre.

"Fine" he concedes.

Just then, the doorbell rings. The girls are dressed head to toe in pink sparkles. Judging by their appearance, I think I could be onto a winner. Abbey seems lovely but starts to cry when she sees the effort I have gone to. David puts his arms around her and mouths out "Thank you" to me. There is lots of squealing when the girl's spot the unicorns sat at the table.

"You need to give them both a name" I tell them. Each one comes with a pretty bracelet with a charm that matches their particular unicorn. "How old are the girls?" I ask Abbey.

"Clara is six and Bluebell is eight," she tells me.

They are very well trained and hang their little cardigans neatly on the back of their chairs.

"Where is Uncle Joseph"? they ask, sounding worried.

Where is Uncle Joseph, I ask myself? I hope he hasn't done a runner. He could be half-way to the pub by now.

"Never mind, we have another visitor at the door. Who can it be?" I say to the girls.

In walks JoJo, the unicorn.

David is practically running to get his phone. Abbey says to me, "Is that him in there?" I quietly nod. Frightened, he might hear us and have a hissy fit. "How did you manage that?" she asks me.

"I had to promise him things in the bedroom department" I confess. She nods. When the girls see him, they both start jumping up and down with excitement.

"I wish Uncle Joseph was here," they both say.

"We'll tell him all about it, later girls," says Abbey.

"JoJo will now sing happy birthday to you, Clara."

We all help him out and join in with the singing. It gets nasty quickly. The girls pull at his tail, so JoJo does one last lap of the kitchen before disappearing through the back door. Abbey, David, and I erupt into fits of laughter.

"What have you done to him?" David jests. "I hardly recognise him."

He is dressed as a pink and white unicorn; I think to myself, what do you expect? I knew exactly what he meant.

"It's all done with hypnosis" I say as I smile at him. "I just tell him to trust me". Joseph soon emerged looking a little worse for wear.

"Damn unicorn head." He moans. "It was so tight I couldn't get it off. I thought it was going to have to be a permanent fixture." I kiss him and push back his now flattened hair from his face. He still looks great. He couldn't have a bad hair day if he tried. I don't think his hair would allow it for a start.

We chat happily and tuck into the food while the girl's play with their unicorns. They call them Toby and Mr Sparkles. "Can we take them to school Mummy?"

"No, but you can wear the bracelets I'm sure". Each one has a charm on it that resembles their own unicorn.

"The bracelets are magic." I tease them. "You touch the picture of your unicorn and it's as if they are stood next to you. Like a guardian angel."

"Is that true Mummy"? I hear Clara ask.

"If Jessie says it is true, then it must be."

I saw it on 'This Morning' so it must be true, I think to

myself.

The men sit in the comfy chairs while Abbey and I tidy up the kitchen. I hear them laughing about what happened on the doorstep yesterday. Joseph calls Abbey to tell her all about it. I walk across and plant a kiss on his lips to silence him. "He could tell you, I say, but then I would have to kill him."

I ask her about her ME. She says she is feeling a bit better, but she is still quite tired. She was supposed to throw a party for Clara, but she didn't feel up to it.

"I like you," she confides to me "try to stick around please".

I smile reassuringly. I decide to confide in her and tell her how smitten I am with Joseph.

"It shows," she tells me. "I couldn't have imagined him dressing up like that for anybody else. You must have really had an effect on him. David had already told me about you too canoodling outside yesterday. To tell you the truth, I think he's a bit jealous. He hasn't had to share him with anyone else before. His old girlfriends didn't seem to hang around for very long."

"Why do you think that was?" I ask, interested.

"He is married to his job. All work and no play make's Joseph a dull boy."

Not a word I would use to describe him. In my eyes, he was anything but.

"He wants kids of his own, you know." She whispers it to me as if it is our secret.

"I know he does, and so do I. Joe junior." I tell her, smiling at the thought.

"Was that his idea or yours"

"Both," I say, "Just a harmless fantasy."

"I see," she replies. "Well, you know what they say, dreams do come true. You need to get married first, though. We've been looking for an excuse to let our hair down." she suddenly says to me.

"How about Christmas eve?"

"Good luck with that one. He's like Bob Cratchit. Come Christmas eve he'll still be working."

He was already talking about working from home, I would have persuaded him to retire by then I think to myself.

Once we are alone, I head upstairs to shower and wait for him in the bedroom. The time has come for me to honour our agreement. A few minutes later he emerges and say's cheekily "Where do you want me?"

Due to our competitiveness of late I decide I will have to make this the best one yet. I suck him long and slow, taking in as much of him as I possibly can. It isn't long before he is making all the right noises. When I sense he is nearing the end, I switch from my mouth to my hand, his buttery voice pleading with me not to stop. Wild horses couldn't stop me, as I'm pretty sure my wrist has gone into spasm and is now working independently. When I am safe in the knowledge that I have procured every last drop, I release my grip on him and watch him make for the bathroom.

When he returns, I am already drowsy.

"Your turn now," he says.

"Just lie next to me."

He walks over and lies down on the bed next to me. As soon as his arms are around me, I feel myself drop off to sleep in the comfort I have made him happy. Which is enough for tonight, anyway?

The Day Trip

The following morning Joseph awakes bright and early. I can hear him plodding around the bedroom, opening blinds and generally faffing about.

"Shopping time" he says excitedly.

I didn't realise he would have me up at the crack of dawn. The shops aren't even open yet. I get up and jump in the shower. He stands silently watching me. I wish he wouldn't do this it unnerves me for some reason. He hands me a towel and stands there watching me again. I am not used to this much scrutiny. I convince him to go and make us both a cup of tea. This should buy me enough alone time to get ready. I finish applying my makeup, douse myself in Chanel, and head downstairs to join him.

He really is in a chirpy mood this morning. He bounces around the kitchen like tigger. He passes me a hot cup of tea and I lean against the kitchen counter and drink it. We need to get going soon. If we want to miss the rush.

"It's bound to be pandemonium in the cushion department" I say to him. Mind you, it usually is when I'm around. It appears we are to be driven by David. Joseph is not paying the man enough; I think to myself. Joseph interprets the look on my face.

"Not that David" he says to me, laughing. There are other ones.

I know this only too well. David Beckham, David Gandy, David Leon to name but a few and throw in Craig David for good measure.

"Besides, I'm flogging him to death at work."

The door-bell rings and David number two's reporting for duty. We climb in the car and are soon speeding up the M3. Metaphorically, that is. He's a very careful driver. Joseph has put one of his best men on the job. We arrive at our destination and hop out of the car. We are both wearing our big coats as the air has turned distinctly cooler. We had been lulled into a false sense of security by the pleasant weather we had been having. I guess it is October.

We stroll across the bridge hand in hand for all the world to see. We glace at each other, now and then, just to exchange the occasional smile. We pass a little café and go inside. We drink tea and munch on shortbread even though we haven't long since had breakfast. All this romantic frivolity is giving me an appetite. We drink-up and start on the next leg of our adventure. We stop now and then just to look in a shop window. Usually shops that sell watches. Yawn. Finally, we are within touching distance of Oxford Street.

By this time, we are both hungry, so we opt to have an early lunch. We haven't bothered to make a booking as we didn't want to tie ourselves down to a fixed schedule. We are going for a gung-ho approach today. Live hard, die young, but never on an empty stomach that was my philosophy. There would always be time for a chocolate bar if nothing else. It might just have to be a Finger of Fudge rather than a king-sized Mars Bar if time was limited.

We are guided to a secluded table towards the back of the restaurant. He is looking at me with those eyes again. Since they are the only ones he has, I guess he doesn't have a choice. Not counting the ones, he has in the back of his head, of course, that can spot a chocolate wrapper at twenty paces or someone searching through a bin to find one. He beckons me towards him as he leans across and whispers in my ear. He tells me exactly what he would like to do to me. As he does this, I know my neck is getting blotchy again. Now he has put the thought in my head I can't get it to leave no matter how hard I try.

The waiter approaches and takes our order. Once he has left, we flirt shamelessly with each other whilst playing footsie under the table. The waiter coughs politely to inform us of his arrival. He places our food down in front of us and makes a quick retreat to the kitchen. We laugh and tuck into our lunch eagerly. He pretends to feed me his food and then takes it away again. That one was getting old, but I still fell for it. He annoys me by trying to make me laugh while I am drinking. I think he is hoping that the liquid will try to escape through my nose. Something I am guilty of trying to do to people I know well. Usually, Robert and I play that little game.

I didn't think we had reached that milestone in our relationship, but it appears we have. I gaze out of the window briefly. He catches me and straight away thinks I must be looking at another man.

"He is about ninety I say in my defence."

"So is Sean Connery, but I bet you wouldn't say no to him." He did have a point.

"He was my favourite Bond," I say to him. "You'd make a good Bond," I joke with him. "You've got the car"

"And the girl," he says to me, "so it's already mission accomplished as far as I am concerned. What would be the point?"

After much deliberation, his, not mine, we order dessert. Chocolate of course in the form of a large sundae and two spoons. He takes hold of my finger and dips it in the silky sauce. He then places it in his mouth and licks the chocolate off seductively. This is conjuring up too far too many memories for me. I twitch again. He tries to carry on, but I pull my finger away as I say, "don't do it again". He seems to get the message as I fan myself. The smile remains on his face for a while.

"I warned you that was what I wanted to do," he says.

"You said a lot of things. I'm glad you stopped at my finger."

"Could have got interesting," he says thoughtfully.

I can see his mind whirring and persuade him to hurry up and get the bill instead. I leave the restaurant along with my friends the red blotch and annoying twitch. Joseph is none the wiser. I don't think he realises the effect he has on me. If he did, then he wouldn't do it. Who am I kidding it would make him do it all the more? The cooling air will hopefully bring my cheeks back to their usual colour. We both have a definite spring in our stride as we turn the familiar corner.

We pass the Palladium and are faced with the familiar black and white building with Liberty emblazoned on the front of it.

"I can buy your Christmas present," says Joseph.

"I thought I knew what you were giving me for Christmas."

"You can have more than one present," he says, smiling broadly.

We skip through the various departments and head up the stairs to homewares. We carefully select a few things to adorn the house and make it a bit of me as he is obsessed that I should feel comfortable when I am there. We loiter in the crockery department. He unwittingly picks up an Alice in Wonderland teacup and saucer and pretends to drink out of it, still being oblivious to how my mind works. Immediately I am transported to David Gandy dressed as the Mad Hatter. An advert I am particularly fond of and have perused the pictures on the internet once or twice. I don't mention my love of all things David Gandy for fear of upsetting him. I don't want a nostril flaring scene in the middle of the store. But I do make a note to self to buy him a top hat.

We leave the warm glow of Liberty and make our way to the shop with the little yellow bags. I have lost him somewhere in the jewellery department and am feeling slightly anxious, like a child that has lost sight of their parent. Eventually thirty minutes later I decide to go and look for him. He is transfixed on a large case of watches. I should have known. It is beginning to feel like a fruitless hunt, as in that old commercial with J.R. Hartley that I have heard about.

I say to him, "No luck then?"

"No" he says to me, looking forlorn.

I start to feel flustered but hide it from him as I spot a small bag in his hand.

"It's just a bracelet," he confesses.

I don't know whether to be pleased or disappointed. I've only known the guy a few days, he is hardly going to be ring shopping.

"Thank you." I say enthusiastically and kiss him on the lips.

Unbeknown to me and as I look away, he sighs in a relieved manner and places the ring box in the pocket of his coat for safe keeping. He already knows this is the one, he just isn't ready to tell her, not just yet.

We walk hand in hand across the bridge we had crossed earlier. We are both carrying a multitude of bags over one free arm. Joseph has called ahead, and David is patiently waiting for us. We do the drive back in silence, but it doesn't feel awkward in the slightest. We are so content in each-other's company already. Another blissful day is almost coming to a close. I mention to him that I should go home and check on things, but he suggests he would like to come with me. I thought he would relish at the thought of alone time away from me, but who am I to argue. If he can't get enough of me, that is his problem.

When we get to the living room, he walks straight over to the piano and starts to tinker with the keys. "I can't leave this alone," he says, "maybe I will have to steal it."

"Maybe I should give it to you," I say, "and the piano!"

"What would you like me to play for you, Jess?"

"I Can't Make You Love Me by George Michael, you probably don't know it, do you?"

"I think I do. Does it sound something like this?"

As he plays, I stand next to him and sing, and as I sing the final line, I start to cry.

"I'm making a habit of it, aren't I?" he tells me, "Making you cry."

I sit down on his lap and hug him for a while. The hug turns into a kiss, but it is not long before we are undressing one another. He sits back down, and I am on top of him with my legs either side of him. I let him enter me again and again as I ride against him. I kiss him on the mouth and stroke his hair.

"We are getting good at this," he says breathlessly.

"Well, you are," I tease him, "I was good already. But you're starting to draw level with me." I say laughing.

Afterwards, I decide to jump in the shower. He follows me and then insists on washing me with a bar of soap. I wonder if he is trying to tell me something, or it is just an excuse to have his hands all over me again. I practically squeak as I walk out of the shower.

We choose to stay at my house tonight. He is without his iPad for once, but it doesn't seem to bother him. We lie in bed drinking tea and eating biscuits. We try to agree on which are the best dunkers while Alexa plays Sam Smith on repeat. Life doesn't get any better, I decide. Sexy voice singing in the background and buttery bits in the bed next to me. Heaven, I think to myself as I suck on his Custard Cream.

"What is on the agenda for tomorrow?" I ask him.

"You might want to sit down for this one," he warns me, "Mum fancies a trip to Wisley Gardens."

"Do you mean the home of the Royal Horticultural Society no less," I say in my poshest voice.

"That's the one," he says in his posher than posh voice. "I guess it's not your thing?" he says, disappointed.

"You're joking aren't you. I love it there. I go there all the time."

"Well, I never," Jess, you do surprise me.

"I must be old before my time, I guess."

"Well, that makes two of us," he says, giving me a smile. "Mum wants to go for lunch, walk around the gardens and then spend lots of money in the plant centre like every other time I've taken her there."

"Sounds good to me," I tell him.

"My two favourite girls together, what a treat."

"I am in your top two then," I say jokingly.

"As long as you don't make me dress up as JoJo, the bloody unicorn!" he says.

I ponder on what I would need to do to move into pole position and make mental notes. Must try even harder next time.

Alone at Last

The next morning, he wakes me up in a panic. "I said we'd pick Mum up at nine, its nearly nine already!"

"Have a quick shower and then I'll jump in after you."

"Won't it be quicker if we both go in there at the same time? Think of the water we could save."

"You know what will happen if we both go in there at the same time. I will drop the bar of soap or you will knock it out of my hand on purpose and I will bend down to pick it up and we will still be there half an hour later. Plus, another two hours to whip me into a frenzy as you pointed out to me."

"You are right, we had better not risk it."

I make tea in a flask and pack pastries in a paper bag for us to eat in the car. By this time, he has finished in the shower. I jump in and out in a record two minutes. Put my hair up and throw on my clothes. We are ready to leave the house at 9:05. Not bad going at all. We rush across the park and hope she is running late.

"I'll start the car," he says, "and you make it look as though we have been waiting for her."

We are becoming like Bonny and Clyde. We are now quite

a formidable double act. It is my job to knock on Celine and John's door and convince her it is her fault we are late. She tells me she will have to cancel. She is having one of her headaches. I think she just wants us to enjoy the time together and is making an excuse. I head back to the car to give Joseph the news.

"We'll go anyway," he says, "you were looking forward to it."

I flash him a smile and say, "I was hoping you would say that. Perhaps we could try that pub by the river afterwards?"

"Good idea," he says, "why didn't I think of that?"

"You've got me now so I can be your ideas person." I say, feeling flushed with my success.

The Porsche flies out of the driveway and along the treelined road. Before long we are on the motorway heading towards the gardens. He has a sexy pair of sunglasses on. It seems strange not to see his eyes for a change. He looks like a different person. We sing along to Life is a Highway by Rascal Flats and other rock classics before pulling into the garden carpark.

I make him take off his glasses by telling him I want to stare into his eyes. He takes them with him, but they are notable by their absence. The leaves are falling from the trees and are landing where the wind carries them. It is still an enjoyable walk around the gardens. We enjoy the greenhouses full of exotic plants. I love orchids so I am in my element as I gaze upon their splendour. We find a bench by the large pond and sit for a while like a couple of old fogies that are lagging. We walk back in the direction of the plant centre. He pushes a trolley and I try my hardest to fill it up with plants.

"You are hoovering the car out when we get back."

"Okay, Mr Grumpy Pants." I say pretending to be upset. I pay for the plants and we head back to the car. He lovingly loads them into the boot for me I am impressed by the meticulous way in which he does it. I quickly get into the car, leaving him to put away the trolley. I just sit and smile at him as he gets in the car.

"I should have left you at home," he says. Pretending to be annoyed. At which point I widen my cat-like emerald eyes and pout. I watch him physically crumble in front of me. He just sighs, shakes his head and drives off. I guess this is one-nil to me then. I pretend to sulk while we drive to the pub.

"I love you really" Joseph say's trying to make it up to me.

"You've got a funny way of showing it," I say, "But I appreciate the sentiment."

By the time we get out of the car, we are friends again. He is all too aware that if I am the cat, he must be the mouse in the relationship. We laugh and chat as we select a table that has the best view out over the lock. It is usually packed to the rafters here at the weekend, but as it is midweek, it is virtually empty. There are a few people making their way along the towpath. In the summer you can't move for people. There is usually an ice-cream van with a large queue stood next to it. I chat enthusiastically about the plants I have purchased.

"You are just like my mum," he says.

"Not too much, I hope?" I enquire.

"I just mean you like the same things."

"Like you, you mean?"

"Well, you both have a great taste in men, what can I say?"

I wasn't about to argue with that. Just then, the food arrives. He has ordered a gourmet burger with all the bells and whistles. I have ordered a lasagne with chips and salad.

"You like big portion's, don't you?" he says to me.

"Don't flatter yourself," I say, teasing him. He laughs and carries on eating his burger. We finish our food and then sit and chat for a while. Watching the world go by.

"This beat's going to work," he says surprising me.

"Maybe I should retire."

"Let's see how you feel at the end of the week shall we?"

"We could become a pair of Gongoozlers." I say to him laughing.

"What on earths that?" He says looking terrified.

I laugh and say, "It is the name for people who love to sit and stare into canals. I find the word amusing, that's all."

"Couldn't I just take up golf like everyone else?"

"Well, we can talk about it nearer the time. There is no rush. You don't have to decide now."

We plan to have an early night, but as we turn the corner and pull into the driveway, we spot David's car parked up. Abbey is sat in the passenger seat beside him. They get out of the car and walk towards us.

"Hey, you too," Abbey says, "Fancy a drink at the pub? We've got rid of the kids for the night so we're at a loose end."

"How did you swing that one?" Joseph asks.

"Inset day tomorrow," David shouts.

"Oh, one of those," Joseph jokes, "What do you think,

Jess?" He turns to face me. "Shall we chance it?"

"I don't see why not," I reply smiling before disappearing inside the house to powder my nose. When I return, I have glammed up a bit and am now wearing my naturally curly hair long and loose. I know Joseph likes it this way, so I shoot him a smile as I walk towards him. He leans out, grabs me with his arm and pulls me to him.

"Hello beautiful girl, fancy a snog?" he mutters in his best peaches and cream voice.

He plants a long lingering kiss on my lips, which makes me tingle inside.

"You've messed up my lipstick," I say to him whilst turning my mouth into a mock frown. What I really want to say is. Watch out, the twitch is back.

"I'll mess up more than that in a minute," he says kissing me again. He hopes he is somehow causing me embarrassment, but these PDA's are just making me love him even more. I'm sure I can walk with my legs crossed if I really try. I glance over at David and Abbey. Abbey is smiling to herself.

"Aw," she says, "isn't it cute."

David on the other hand is looking serious. He breaks into

a smile when he notices me watching him.

"Isn't it just," he says, trying to paint a fake smile on his face just for my benefit. There is something about the way he said that comment that makes me feel uneasy. I decide to push it firmly to the back of my mind for the time being. I was determined not to let anything spoil this evening.

We do a bit of a pub crawl. David and Abbey take Joseph up on his offer to sleep in his spare room tonight.

"I'll let you work from home tomorrow if you like?" he says to David. "I am the boss, and you have to do as I say, remember."

David looks irritated by Joseph's words but smiles. I can sense something is bubbling up between them. I don't know if it is just my feminine intuition up to its old tricks again.

Abbey walks beside me while the boys walk in front. They appear to be winding each other up about something. Friendly banter, one might call it. Abbey reads my mind and says, "Ignore them. They are always like this. It's like a game to see who can wind the other one up the most." She pauses before saying, "We can see how happy the two of you are. We think its lovely."

"David doesn't mind me stealing Joseph away from him

then?" I ask her.

"I'd say you are doing him a favour. It's given him more time to spend with me and the girls. He actually read them a bedtime story the other night. We had an early night for the first time in ages, thanks to you, and it was perfect. The kids now fall asleep straight away, clutching their unicorns. Those unicorns have been a complete godsend. We pretend that Toby and Mr Sparkles are telling them to go to bed early and it works like a dream. Bluebell has even opened up to us about what has been bothering her at school. It turns out Toby her best friend has got himself a girlfriend. Bluebell has decided it doesn't matter. She is done with men, anyway."

What a wise girl she is, I think to myself although; I had been ready to give it all up when I met Joseph that would have been a waste.

"Besides, she has new Toby now. He is a much more impressive version than the old one. He even sparkles and has a tail."

Joseph has a rather impressive tail; I think to myself and smile at the thought of it. "That's great," I say, "I am happy to have been of assistance."

"You're a regular Mary Poppins in our house, I can tell you." she confides, "It's Jess this and Jess that. They even eat vegetables now as you told them they are a unicorn's favourite food. I'm just in complete awe at your abilities."

It's a shame her husband doesn't feel the same way. I ponder and felt better. Maybe I imagined it all. It sounds as if I am worrying myself unnecessarily. He is Joseph's closest friend. How could he be anything but nice if Joseph is so fond of him, it makes little sense?

We arrive at the first pub in the village. It might be a small village, but it has about five or six pubs. It must have been designed by a man.

"Shall we go in this one?" Joseph says.

"It would be rather rude not to," we say laughing.

We walk in and find a table where we can be as raucous as we want to be and still not upset anyone. Abbey and I sit down while the boys fetch the drinks. I settle on a cocktail, a Long Island Iced Tea, to be more specific. The boys return with the drinks, which are accompanied by an array of snacks to soak up the alcohol. David and Abbey begin making eyes at each other across the table. Joseph, not wishing to be outdone leans across the table and kisses me tenderly on the lips. We allow our gaze to just sit and rest on each other for a while. We retreat into a secret world of our own as this happens.

"I must say," Joseph says, "You two are looking happy. Aren't they Jess?" I nod my head.

"We actually got an early night last night." Abbey whispers.

"Did you?" Joseph says in an accusing voice. "That explains the grin on his face. I'm happy for you," he continues. "It's worked wonders for me. All these early nights Jess and I have been having. I feel like a new man!"

You'd better not, I think to myself. Hazel would never let me live it down if she'd been right about that. Another direct hit for her 'gaydar'. We finish our drinks and head off in search of the next pub. Abbey and David walk in front whilst Joseph and I walk slowly behind, happily swinging our hands as we walk. His blue eyes are lighting up like the night sky as they stare into mine. I have the voice of Gary Barlow in my head telling me we can rule to world.

"You look really beautiful tonight," he says proudly. "I love your hair like that," he coos.

"I know you do. Why do you suppose I'm wearing it like this? It's all for you baby," I confess to him.

He stops suddenly, takes my face in his hands and kisses me so passionately on the lips that when he lets go, I almost fall over.

"Oops," he steadies me and laughs. "I must be getting too good at kissing as well. I thought I would try remove a bit of lipstick I didn't get off the first time."

"Thank you." I tell him, "You're always thinking of me."

"You know me too well," he replies grinning. We join hands again and just as we are about to catch up Abbey and David, I ask Joseph if he thinks David likes me.

"Why wouldn't he? You come with a list of credentials as long as your arm. He hasn't stopped banging on about you all evening. He thinks you're great and far too good for me."

"Okay that's good," I say feeling a bit more convinced.

"You're not thinking of running off with him, are you?" He asks sounding jealous.

At which point, I look at him and say, "Why would I go out for a burger when I can have steak at home? A nice juicy one like you."

"Does this mean you love me?" He says trying to sound adoringly vulnerable.

"I should bloody hope so. The number of awkward scrapes you have got me into this week. They are really starting to add up!"

"I guess you must love me then," he says, making eyes at me.

We arrive at the next pub on the hit list. We go in and locate a table, this time Abbey and I get the drinks in while David and Joseph have a quick game of pool. "I genuinely have never seen Joseph this loved up," she confides in me.

"I've not felt like this before either. I've kissed a lot of frogs in my time," I tell her.

"Haven't we all?" she says in reply.

I smile at the barman as he hands us our drinks and walk across the pub to our table. Joseph and David are busy flicking beer mats at each other.

"You took so long with the drinks we got bored," as if it defends their child-like behaviour.

"We can't help it if there is a queue. Anyway, that's no excuse for acting like a couple of toddlers," Abbey says looking annoyed.

"Sorry Ab's, Joseph says I won't do it again."

David pipes up, "You were having a moment with that barman just now, Jess." His grin broadening as he says it.

Abbey jumps to my defence, "I didn't notice that, and I was there! He was just friendly, that's all."

"Extremely friendly," David says, trying to make something out of nothing.

Joseph's nostrils flare at the suggestion, but he still retains a faint smile on his face. Although, it is growing weaker by the second.

"We could hear you winding Joseph up about something," says Abbey. She touches my arm and says, "Ignore him. He's just jealous. He always has been."

"Well, Peter Perfect does seem to have it all," David snipes.

"You do too," Abbey says, pinching his cheeks. "You have quite a lot to be thankful for if my memory of last night serves me correctly."

"Don't tell us anymore," begs Joseph. "Don't tell me anything I can't unsee."

We laugh and enjoy our drinks. I get that uneasy feeling again as David meets my gaze across the table. I can't decide if it is just mock sibling rivalry between the two of them or something much worse. I push it to the back of my mind again. It's nothing, I convince myself. Stop being so stupid.

We decide to order more drinks. Abbey politely declines

and say's "Not for me," she is already giggling like an idiot.

"Lightweight!" David shouts at her. He jumps up and says, "I'll get these."

When he returns from the bar, he tells me "I thought I'd get you something else to try," with a mad look in his eyes. "It may even put hairs on your chest."

"Don't drink it, Jess, not if you don't want to." Abbey says protectively.

I am used to drinking doubles on my pub nights with Andrew, so how bad could it be? David and Joseph egg me on by banging on the table. I neck it and shout "Down the hatch!" as I place the glass up to my lips. It must have been a triple. It burns my throat and makes me shiver as it goes down. I make an excuse and head to the ladies. I stop at the bar and ask the barman what he had put in my drink?

"Triple Vodka. Nothing else. I was watching him the entire time. He seems a bit off, I'd keep an eye on him if I were you."

I nod and carry on to the ladies. I look back to see Joseph staring at me. He doesn't look pleased. David's lies ringing in his ears. All the incessant jealousy is getting to me. I wasn't used to all the insecurity he was displaying. I was feeling out of my depth as we make our journey back to the house. I couldn't help but wonder what his problem is. He is handsome, rich and seemingly has it all there must be something going on that I don't yet know about.

Joseph is very quiet, which is not like him at all. "What were you and that barman talking about earlier?" he asks me.

"Nothing really, I was just trying to find out what was in my drink."

"It was only a single vodka," he says, laughing.

"Triple actually, according to the barman."

He gives me a look of surprise.

"It was probably just David's idea of a joke to get you legless, Jess. I might take advantage of that later," he says, winking at me.

"I'm counting on it," I say, shooting him a sexy smile.

The walk takes a little longer than it did earlier as we are all swaying a little due to the fresh air mixing with the alcohol and muddling our brains. We think about getting chips but decide not to bother as we are nearly home now. Joseph gently pushes me against a nearby wall and kisses my neck. We both felt breathless and giddy. I hang my arms around his neck and gaze into his eyes longingly. I plant a few open-mouthed kisses on his perfect lips and shudder slightly as I feel him harden against me.

"I wish I didn't have to stop. It hurts, I want you so much."

"It looks as if it might be painful!" I say laughing.

"I want you too!" I say to him, "But our audience awaits so you are going to have to hold that thought."

Abbey and David are watching us from the top of the road. "Come on, then." I say and grab his hand so we can catch up with the others.

Joseph has not one, not two, but three attempts at getting the key in the lock, in the end Abbey grabs it from him and pushes him out of the way.

"Here, let me do it silly boy," she says affectionately. She has her legs crossed as she is dying for the loo. We all try to pile over the threshold at the same time and end up in a heap in the hallway. Which makes us laugh even more. Joseph is already half-way up the stairs with Abbey following behind. I decide to go to the kitchen to get a glass of water. I fiddle around with the tap for a while, trying to get the water as cold as possible as I am hoping it will help to counteract my fuzziness. It takes a minute or two to cool down. I can feel his arms around me as he kisses the back of my neck. "I didn't hear you come downstairs," I say as I turn to look at him.

It is not the beautiful eyes I am used to. David is stood behind me. With a mad look on his face. I try to walk away, but he blocks my path.

"What are you doing?" I bark at him, my heart beating hard in my chest.

"What I've been wanting to do all evening," he says sneering at me.

I push his hands away and run up the stairs. But he follows behind me.

"I hope you know what you are getting in to with him. Maybe you and Celine can carry on with the babysitting, freeing me up to do what I should be doing, looking after the company rather than the 'go-to' man."

I close the bedroom door and slip into bed next to a now snoring Joseph. A tear runs down my cheek at the thought of what has just happened. How could he do that to Abbey and the kids? Joseph even, or me come to that? Maybe there is more to his behaviour than pure jealousy? I pull the duvet tightly around me and close my eyes to make it all go away.

Time to Forget

In the morning I fake a hangover and stay in bed until I hear the Range Rover pull away. I have a long shower to wash away the feel of him. But it lingers. Joseph tries to join me, but I lie to him and tell him I have a headache. He looks disappointed but says he understands. He smiles and says enthusiastically, "How about some breakfast then?"

"Great" I tell him.

"A good breakfast that's all you need," he says from downstairs. If only. I think to myself. And something to wipe my memory. As I am walking down, I can hear him banging about in the kitchen. He hasn't got a clue where anything is, even in his own house. I caught him yesterday trying to find the toaster which had been sat there staring at him from the spot where it has always been, presumably.

Even a hot shower could not wash away the memory of last night. I had hoped to wash it down the drain along with the remainder of the soap. I tried to make light of the situation for my own sake. "What's cooking good looking?" I say, trying to sound a bit happier than I felt.

"Corn flakes," he says, passing me a grim-looking bowl for me to try.

"Just think," I say to him, "when you get good at this cooking lark, we can get you all your own kitchen accessories and we can stamp your name on them, twice even if you like."

"You mean Joseph Joseph don't you. I get it."

He usually catches up in the end, but it sometimes takes a while.

"You're not just a pretty face after all," I say, teasing him. "Let's head out and get breakfast instead."

"Good idea," he says grabbing his keys and heading for the door. We drive over to the Old School Café which sits just outside the village. We step inside where there is a group of women all scurrying around like worker bees to feed the hungry white-van drivers sat and waiting to be served. We walk up a couple of steps to a more secluded part of the café. It has large windows looking out over the main road and fields beyond.

"David and Abbey enjoyed themselves last night," He says cheerily. "David was full of beans this morning. He put it down to a good night's sleep."

He and Abbey are off for a jolly somewhere. "Oh, nice" I say, trying to sound happy.

He gets to go off on a Jolly Boy's outing while I'm left

feeling like crap with his clueless best mate.

"You've made a good impression on him despite your reservations," he says.

Luckily, the food arrives. As I'm sick of the conversation. A lovely full English. This will take my mind off David for a while at least.

I picture his nasty face as I stab my sausage with my fork. After we have finished up inside, we head back to the car and go for a drive. Let's just go where the wind takes us are Joseph's words. He is wearing his sunglasses again. His killer smile never leaving his face as the wind tousles his hair through the partially open sunroof. Apple CarPlay banging out his favourite tunes. I try to sing along, but the memory of recent events takes over and taints everything. Turning everything a depressing shade of black. How dare he do this? If push came to shove, I wouldn't hesitate to throw him under the proverbial bus. A couple of times if necessary and then reverse back over him just to make sure. I decide to park it for the moment and enjoy the day.

Andrew and I were members of the National Trust, so I still have both our membership cards in my purse. We drive to Winkworth Arboretum as it is fairly close. If there is a problem with the card, I will just blag it if necessary. Show them my bottom as it's worked for me so far.

On arrival, it looks as if we have swapped Surrey for New England in the fall. Beautiful trees adorn the place in every autumnal colour of the spectrum. A firework display of leaves and foliage goes off all around us. I slip away into my own thoughts as we walk hand in hand through the splendour. We wander over to a bench and sit down. We are situated on the edge of a large grassy area. The outer perimeter is filled with every kind of specimen tree you can imagine. We sit and fantasise this is our plot of land we have just purchased in order to build our dream home. We sit and plan it down to the last detail. A large sweeping drive will lead up to a cutting edge, architect-designed house that is flooded with light due to the huge expanses of glass on all sides. After completion, we will fill the house with purchases from Dwell that will give it the contemporary edge that we are hoping for.

It will feature on the cover of 25 Beautiful Homes alongside a carefully written narrative given on how we created the dream. We have even picked the tree from which a swing for Joe Junior will be hung as a Labrador or two chase a ball in the distance.

When we are done with daydreaming, we continue our walk. There are lots of steps to climb during which we have the realisation that we are not as fit as we thought we were. He is still as fit as ever but I, on the other hand, am breathless, and this time, not in a good way. We are now back at the entrance which overlooks the cafe so we conclude it would be bad of us not to have a cream tea. I pick a table in a quiet corner and sit down.

Just as I have started to forget my problems Joseph's phone rings and David's name pops up on the screen. He has left it on the table while he goes back inside to get the sugar. I feel sick to the stomach and wish he would just leave us alone. He'd done what he set out to do. To try to break us up, that is. I decide not to tell Joseph about the call, maybe he won't notice but he hears it ringing and hurries back to answer it. He walks over to a grassy area to take the call. When he returns, I ask if everything is okay?

"Yes, fine," he answers, "work stuff. Nothing for you to worry your pretty little head about," he says, stroking my cheek gently with his hand.

Let me be the judge of that, I think to myself. We tuck into our scones, jam, and clotted cream. Just as I put mine to my lips, ready to devour it, he jogs me so that I end up with cream and jam all over the end of my nose. I tut and tell him not to be so childish. I then do the same thing to him, so he is covered in it as well. At least he doesn't try to lick it off this time. We don't want to put people off their food.

We contemplate a stroll around nearby Godalming but decide that we have had enough walking for that day, which is ironic because as soon as we get home one of the first things; we do is head out to take Eric and Ernie for a walk. We energetically chase the dogs around the park. I am playing with one of those ball firing contraptions. They take it in turns to run for the ball. Joseph meanwhile decides to get on all fours and pretend to be a dog just to add more spice to the mix. I throw jellybeans in the air as he moves about, catching them in his mouth as I shower him with praise and tickle his tummy. How far we have come in such a short space of time. I feel as though our relationship has reached real maturity.

The air turns cooler suddenly, so we gather up the boys and head back. We make the short journey that I have begun to know and love so much. The Lodge house is beginning to feel like home to me too, especially as all of our Liberty purchases are now dotted around the house. I will embellish it a little more over time. After all, there is no rush. It is only my second home, after all. Once the dogs have been dropped off to their mum and dad, we have a little stroll around the garden. We are filled with giddy nostalgia as we make our way back across the perfectly manicured lawns.

The phone rings and yet again it is David. Joseph heads along the hallway to his study. Usually, I would have felt irritated at this, but I just felt relieved instead. I am pleased to have the temporary feeling of peace, to be perfectly honest. I head into the kitchen to make us both a cup of tea. I arrange a selection of his favourite biscuits on a plate and take it to his study. As I make my approach, I am treated to David's dulcet tones on speaker coming from within. His slimy voice begins to turn my stomach. How different it is to Josephs buttery vernacular, which I never tire of hearing. I can hear David saying,

"Kick her out if she's annoying you. Filling your house with all her tat."

"It's not tat, I never said that. I just need to get in touch with my feminine side, that's all. I'm just not used to it feeling like a home."

"Yeah right!" David snaps.

Joseph swallows hard as he spots me in the doorway. Embarrassment written all over his face. I put down his tea and biscuits and leave the room.

"Looks as if you have got her well trained?" David continues trying to provoke an argument.

"I've lucked out completely. All she wants to do is love and care for me. Who am I to argue?" he tells an increasingly irritated David.

When he has finished his call, he comes back to join me in the kitchen. "He is only messing about," Joseph says trying to defend David's nasty comments.

"Please don't take it so personally, Jess. I will have a word with him next time I speak to him if it makes you feel better?"

"Maybe I am taking over your house and filling it with crap?" I say to him. "Perhaps I should go back to my own house if that is easier? It won't take me five minutes to get my 'tat' together."

"Please don't talk like that. I'm liking all this 'crap' of yours. It's starting to grow on me." He has a knack of saying the right thing at the right time, I was lucky to have him and I knew it. We fall into bed and drift off to sleep without our usual bedtime activities. We are both shattered from the couple of late nights we have had. I'm also not in the mood for anything too strenuous anymore. David has made sure of that.

What Comes Next

When I wake up, Joseph is still snoozing in bed. I can't shake off David's words or actions, come to that. I think about telling Joseph everything but decide it is better not to mention it yet. I thought David and Abbey liked me. After all, I threw their daughter a birthday party, but I guess I was wrong. I don't want to stir up trouble between them. I have not been around long enough yet to allow myself to cause that devastation.

I creep downstairs to make myself breakfast. Just as I reach the kitchen, Joseph's phone rings. Three guesses who that is, I think to myself. The proverbial pantomime villain. Joseph waves to me as he walks past. He is retreating to his study to talk about me again; I expect. I take a shower and get dressed. Alan has asked if I can pop into work for a bit to help him out with something, so I get ready, grab a spare cardboard box to pack up my stuff and head down to let Joseph know I am needed at work.

He is speaking to David on speaker phone while he frantically hunts through a drawer for paperwork. They are both due to attend a meeting with Alan this morning to discuss requirements for the upcoming stock orders, after which Joseph and I are planning to have lunch together. I can hear Joseph and David having an argument. It seems considerably more heated this time. I can hear David shouting.

"What are you doing? You hardly know her, for god's sake. Anyway," he continues, "you know she made a pass at me that night after the pub?"

"You're lying!" Joseph says trying his best to defend me.

"So, what if I am? I'm trying to help you see sense. You were only looking for fun, but you've practically moved her in. I still don't think you're in the right head space."

"I have had all I can take of your so-called friend. A gut full, in fact!" I shout at him through the door. I am completely raging as I pick up the part-packed box and slam the door behind me.

His watch is due to be delivered this morning. Now I have to go into work, and I won't be around to sign for it. I'm leaving him and I can't even say goodbye. As I head across the park, the tears come thick and fast. I wish I hadn't gone for a walk in the park that day. I could have saved myself a shedload of heartache.

I jump in my car, feeling like my whole world has come

crashing down around me. He's supposed to be meeting Alan soon, so I guess I will catch up with him then. I'm just glad I have not gotten around to introducing him to my family yet. I wanted to be certain about him first. What I was certain of is that he is a complete 'bell-end', 'nob', 'arsehole' or all of the above!

I arrive at work and park a little way down the road, hoping he won't realise I'm here or knock my wingmirrors off in a fit of rage. I can always dive under the desk and hide, I guess.

11:30 comes and goes, but there is still no sign of him. He was supposed to be bringing Nigel for an outing so, even if I hadn't seen him, I would have heard his arrival. I venture upstairs in trepidation just in case he has donned his superman costume and flown here instead. I wrack my brain. He must be running late, as usual. There are only a few of us in today, as there seems to be a lot of staff off sick at the moment. It is just the select few who are due to sit in on the meeting, and they all turn to look at me as I walk in.

Alan is looking particularly pensive. He is pacing back and forth for some reason. As he puts the phone down, he beckons me over to his office and I get a distinct feeling that something is wrong. Don't tell me Joseph has asked him to fire me. That really would take the biscuit. As I sit down, he explains in a calm voice that he has just got off the phone to Celine.

"I have been trying to get hold of Joseph without any luck." Says Alan.

What am I, his babysitter now I think to myself? Although David had joked about that.

I sit there bemused; I am still waiting for the punchline.

"I don't know if he told you, but we brought the meeting forward by an hour to 10:30. David hadn't been able to reach him either, so he called Celine to go to the house and check on him."

It's about time he did something useful for a change.

"She got there just in time. He'd tried to kill himself, by all accounts."

I just stare at him for a long moment in disbelieve. "Is he going to be okay?" I ask him.

"We don't know, he was unconscious, and the doctor is in attendance. Celine is yet to speak to him."

I sit there in silence, not knowing what to say.

"She tried to get hold of you, but you weren't picking up your phone. Yours was the last number he tried to call."

I look at my phone and see three missed calls. I feel as if

I'm going to pass out. I've been in such a state that I haven't even looked at my phone in the last few hours.

"We had an argument this morning, so I didn't want to talk to him." I then tell Alan about the phone conversation I'd overheard, including David accusing me of making a pass at him, even though the truth was the exact opposite.

"I don't know David that well, but I know Joseph would not believe those things, he's nuts about you. He told me that when I spoke to him yesterday. I think you should drop what you are doing and go straight to him and don't worry about anything to do with work at the moment. Please call me as soon as possible to tell me everything is Okay"

I run back to my car and drive towards home. Part of the way there, I need to pull over and stop in a lay-by. Sam Smiths Lay Me Down is on my play list. It comes on and I finally lose it. We were only listening to it a couple of days ago; we were so happy! 'F… You' David!

I start to feel a numbness come over me. I am feeling really light-headed, as if I'm going to pass out. I check my pulse and I can no longer feel it, my heart is beating so fast. I know the drill; I have to really concentrate on slowing down my breathing before I lose consciousness. I force myself to breathe slowly and deeply. Sometimes it takes a while for everything to return to normal.

My panic attack is in full swing now there is nothing I can do to stop it. I carry on using the breathing technique I have taught myself. I check my pulse and it is beginning to return to normal, but I still have a feeling of pins and needles in my arm. I can't lose him. Life without him is not an option anymore. That horse has well and truly bolted. He was the one thing keeping me going and getting me through.

Just then my phone rings. It is the delivery company trying to drop off his watch. I tell them to wait, I am just around the corner and will be there in a couple of minutes.

I come to a screeching halt outside my house and run to the front door to sign for the delivery. I go inside and sit down on the sofa with the unopened box in my hand when I decide to open it to have a closer look inside. I can see exactly why he wanted it so much. The gold dial and detailing are beautiful. I just hope and pray I will get to deliver it to him.

I leave the house and head for the park. I have left the watch at home for safekeeping as I'm not sure I will be a welcome visitor at the house, but I need to be there if and when he wakes up. I don't care if he never wants to see me again, I just need to know how he is. I can't help thinking that this is all my fault somehow. I should have read the signs.

Having had anxiety and panic attacks, I should have known exactly what to lookout for. His strange behaviour combined with the jealousy and mood swings. His vulnerability. Celine did say he has been depressed but, I can't help but wonder, if he has done this before. I suddenly realise Celine and David have been on suicide watch. It is all starting to click into place.

I can see Celine stood on the driveway. Her shoulders are going up and down with each sob. I run over to her and put my arms tightly around her. We embrace for a good while, both of us completely overcome with emotion.

"Don't blame yourself," she says generously, "This isn't your fault. He has been unhappy for a while now, and something just pushed him over the edge. Since you came along, Jess, he had been back to his old self and it felt like we got our son back. I honestly thought we'd seen the worst of it. I know all about what David has been saying, Alan told me just now. I'm sorry you had to go through that. This could have been enough to send Joseph into a downward spiral."

They had sold me a house with an unexploded bomb in the basement. Why hadn't someone trusted me enough to tell me what was going on? I could have done something, helped him or gone with him to see a counsellor. Anything would have been easier than this.

"That's why you put the tracker on his phone, isn't it? You didn't trust him. Has he attempted this before?" I ask her.

She looks at me shiftily. "Yes. I found him that time as well. Just by chance and just in time. He was a bit more determined to get the job done on that occasion. We got him checked out at the hospital and professional help. It seemed to work and gradually he got better."

"You shouldn't have to carry the burden alone," I say to her gently.

"John helps in his own way," says Celine.

Her loyalty to the end was admirable. Just then the doctor emerges from the house and summons us. Celine looks frail as she walks over to him, so I hold her arm for support.

"How's he doing, doctor?" Celine asks.

"Shaken, but stable. He's going to need lots of rest. He has given himself a bit of a shock. I think it was just an honest mistake. Drank too much and then took pain killers but only a few. He had dropped most of them on the floor as he reached for them. It wasn't as bad as we all first thought. But I can understand your thought process after the last time. He'll mend. He just needs lots of TLC and I am guessing I can rely on you two ladies to give him that. He has had something to make him sleep so he will be out for a couple of hours, so I suggest you two go and get something to eat. You will have a period of hard work ahead."

"Thank you, doctor." says Celine.

I smile and thank him for all his help. At least he is going to be okay. Thank god. Relieved, we cross the road and walk to Anton's. We will be careful what we say so as to not alert the village gossips. That is the last thing any of us need. We grab sandwiches and a drink and head to the park. We have bought lavender shortbread for later to have with a pot of tea. We don't say very much as we sit on the bench and eat our lunch, but I can tell Celine is grateful of the company.

"I've got the watch he's been looking for. I found a stockist that had one and it arrived earlier today."

"Oh, you silly girl. What made you do that. It must have cost a fortune?" she says shaking her head.

"It's worth every penny, just to make him happy. I love him so much, it hurts."

"Well," she says touching my arm, "I know exactly how that feels!"

We cry again, but with relief this time. She changes the subject.

"You wait till I get my hands-on David. I have a good mind to send him packing. We have been so good to him over the years, and this is how he repays us by upsetting our boy so much that he does this to himself. I was never sure about him and now, 1 know why. Pretending to be Joseph's friend while all the time plotting his downfall. That must be a bloody big chip he's carrying on his shoulder, I can tell you, and to think we treated him like family. You're more like family than he is. Or I hope you will be one day, anyway."

She stops and falls silent for a few moments, realising she may be over-reacting.

"On reflection, maybe I have been asking too much of him. He has been monitoring Joseph at the office. I guess he has had enough. Maybe he was feeling like a spare part and slightly threatened now you are around."

"I didn't mean to cause any trouble; I just want to be part of his life."

"You, darling girl, have nothing to apologise for. You're like the daughter I never had. The daughter I wish I had." She says hugging me again. "We need to be positive. He is going to need to rely on both of us from now on." She says trying to sound stronger than she is.

We take a few deep breaths and head back to the house.

The doctor is just leaving as we get there. We tidy the house for no particular reason. It seems like a good way for us both to pass the time. We make tea and sit and munch on lavender shortbread. A bit of sugar is just what we need right now. David turns up at the house. Celine is enraged and goes outside to have a few choice words with him. I watch him saunter to his car and drive away. I don't know what she said to him, but it worked. She is something else. I can see why she means so much to Joseph. She means a lot to me already, and I haven't known her very long.

When she comes back, she says "I wasn't very ladylike I'm afraid, but I think he got the message loud and clear."

We both laugh.

"We don't need men to do the dirty work, we can do it ourselves. Boy, that felt good." she says, "I think I taught him a few extra words today. Serves him right. If he takes on one of us, he takes on all of us, don't you think?"

"I think you are amazing." I say to her.

She smiles back at me and say's "So are you."

It has reached the time when the doctor said Joseph would start to stir. I decide it is only right to let Celine see him first. She is not going to mention that she has seen me. She will let that be a surprise.

As I dash back across the road to get the box, I grab a few moments for myself. I tidy up my face and walk back to the Joseph's house. I stand outside and wait for Celine to come back down. It's a good ten minutes before she re-emerges looking red eyed and drained of all emotion.

"Your turn, darling," she says to me.

I take a deep breath and quietly climb the stairs. The bedroom door is still closed but I will not be flinging it open and shouting surprise that is for sure. I will be far too emotional for that. I slowly open the door. He seems to be lost in thought. He hasn't even noticed me. He is sat on the edge of the bed and I think he is still crying. I go to him, trying to keep it all together, but as soon as I see him, I fall down at his feet and hold on to him. The tears will not stop now they just keep coming. He clings on to me as I stroke his hair.

I move away to look at him. His eyes, no longer bright, show the pain that has taken control of him. I stroke his face and kiss his mouth. I think about giving him a hard time but, how can I? I think he has suffered enough.

"I'm so sorry I wasn't here when you needed me. You know you can always talk to me, about anything." I say to him. "If I'd lost you? Well, it doesn't bear thinking about. You are part of me now. Two halves of the same coin." I say and smile at him through my tears.

He smiles faintly at me, but his eyes are still sad.

"You know none of that stuff David said about me was true, don't you?" I sobbed.

"He admitted as much. He also told me about his inappropriate behaviour whilst being drunk. He wasn't proud of it!" explains Joseph. "So, I just lost it completely. I threatened to do all sorts to him, I was so angry. You should have told me straight away. I would have decked him, there and then, and thrown him out of the house. Not let him stick around for a cosy sleepover."

"Let's forget about him. Anyway, I have a surprise for you."

"Last time you said that it was a magical unicorn costume."

"Not this time. You're going to like this one, I promise. Lie down on the bed, close your eyes and hold out your hands. Just do it." I say to him. He does as he is told, and I place the box in his hands. He opens his eyes and looks at me.

"What is this?"

"Just open it already." I say getting impatient.

He opens the lid and smiles from ear to ear. His eyes

shining a little brighter now.

"It is the right one, isn't it? The one you've been searching for?" I ask nervously.

"Yes, you are." He says with tears in his eyes.

Time to Heal

I open my eyes hesitantly and gaze across at him. He is now blissfully sleeping next to me like a baby. Totally oblivious to the turmoil that he has instilled within me. I just stare at his beauty for a while, thankful that I am still able to do so. I tell myself, from this moment on, I will dedicate my every waking moment to his needs and wellbeing. He has been told that he must take it easy and get lots of rest and fresh air. So, I decide to stay in bed with him. I just want to be close to him, even if he is oblivious to me.

I read books and magazines, drink endless cups of tea and eat countless biscuits. I start to worry that I will be too fat to get out of bed soon and it is only day one. Who knows how many more days like this there will be? I decide to get up, walk about and clear my head. I walk over to the window and just look out to the walled garden and reflect on our perfect alfresco encounter. We have already had so many perfect days it would be difficult to pick one. Who knows? Maybe the best is yet to come.

I start to poke around in his wardrobes and marvel at how amazingly organised he is. I imagine our future trips to Ikea. I visualise the arguments when we realise, we can't fit our purchases into the boot of the car. I smile as I open a drawer and just as I do so I hear him coming up behind me.

"What are you doing" he asks, sounding flustered.

"Just poking around in your drawers. Do you have a problem with that?" I ask.

I sense there is something in that wardrobe of his that he doesn't want me to see. So, I close the drawer and quietly move away.

"Sorry," I say to him, "I was getting bored."

"Speaking of poking around in drawers, why don't I run us a nice bath and maybe I can have a poke around in yours. What do you say?" he says, waiting for me to reply.

I just smile and say, "Your wish is my command. I am here in a sex slave capacity to attend to your every wish."

"Wish you would hurry up and rub my lamp," he says, running to the bathroom.

Despite the verbal foreplay, we both climb in the bath and just chat happily with each-other. It feels just like it had before, but better somehow. I now know the type of man I am dealing with. When we get out of the bath, our urges get the better of us. We fall on the bed and make long lingering love. My legs wrapped tightly around him in an embrace. We kiss and stroke one another's faces while he plunges in and out of me. Afterwards, he collapses on top of me and gets me to stroke his hair. We need no words to convey how the other one is feeling. We know each-others thought process so well now. Maybe even too well.

We decide to invite Celine and John to spend the evening with us. Joseph hasn't seen either of them since it happened. We choose to make pizza, or rather I do, and dust off my favourite Paul Hollywood recipe. Joseph will give me a hand with the toppings. Surely, he can't do too much damage.

I'm hoping to see his moves in the kitchen he had spoken about. Instead, he just generally arses about throwing flour at me and making a mess of the place. Finally, we get everything prepared just as the doorbell rings. Everyone else sits down while I faff about in the kitchen cooking pizzas, making salads, and generally running around like a headless chicken. I lay everything out prettily on the table in the conservatory. I even light a few scented candles, hoping to create a bit of ambience. Lavender, of course. Pizza Express eat your heart out, I think to myself as I put on subtle background music. I don't really know John and Celine's taste in music. Alexa had already lost her temper with me when I couldn't decide what I wanted her to play. In the end she said in a tired voice, "What do you want me to play?" Even she is sick of my inability to make decisions.

I finally decide on a bit of David, Craig David that is. Everyone likes Craig David, right? I'm sure when he belts out 'Bo' and 'Selecta' Celine will know exactly where he is coming from. I turn it down, so it is just background noise rather than full on Ibiza set, which is how I usually like to listen to it. As we sit down and eat our food, we chat easily about our day and plans for the coming days. Celine has spent most of hers in bed, but that was to be expected as she was looking done-in when I said goodbye to her yesterday. She looks a bit more like her old self now.

The food goes down a storm, and I clear the dishes and collect dessert from the kitchen. I have heated up one of Anton's cherry pies as I know it is a family favourite. I put a jug of hot custard and ice-cream down on the table. There are appreciative moaning noises coming from the other guests as they tuck into their cherry pie. Celine and John take it in turns to yawn and tell us they really should be getting back as they need to let the dogs out before bed. It is her subtle way of letting us have time to ourselves.

Joseph and I stand at the front door with our arms around each-other waving goodbye to them.

"Right," Joseph says, "how about a horror movie as it is

Halloween in a week or so? There's bound to be a late night Spooktacular on somewhere."

He flicks through the channels and finds something I've never even heard of. It is full of bangs and loud noises that seem to frighten the hell out of me. My least favourite film genre possible. At least I get to cuddle up to Joseph, even if I have my eyes closed most of the time.

"I am not locking up tonight," I say to him.

He just laughs in a mimic of Dracula's voice. At last, the film finishes, and I can relax again. As I head into the kitchen to get a glass of water I am reminded of David. The last thing I want is someone creeping up behind me now. I am relieved not to feel unwanted breath on the back of my neck. I am just finishing up when there is a loud banging on the kitchen window.

I shout, "F... ME!" in a very loud voice.

I look up to see Joseph disappearing into one of the flower beds. He is laughing so much that he has lost his footing and has almost face planted. You would think he would remember from the last time he banged on my car window. I rush up to bed, leaving him to lock up, deciding to hide behind the bedroom door and jump out on him. We have resorted to behaving like children again, so everything must be getting back to normal. He literally jumps ten foot in the air, and I am on my knees unable to stand, I am laughing so much. I get into bed and pretend to be intellectual by attempting the telegraph crossword. I have my glasses on and keep pausing and pondering as if I am waiting for an answer to come to me. I have actually already given up, but I don't want to turn the light out just yet as I haven't recovered from my fright earlier. He is playing solitaire on his iPad just for a change.

"What you said earlier," he says smiling, "did you mean it?"

I can't work out what he is talking about. I give him a confused look. When I was at the kitchen window. He's referring to the 'F… ME' incident.

He says, "Put a please on the end and we might have a deal."

He turns the light out and undresses me. Suddenly I'm not afraid anymore; of anything.

Next Stop Greenway

The next morning, we both wake up bright and early. Yet another sunny day is here to greet us. It's hard to believe it was only this time last week we were waking up together for the first time. So much has happened in seven days that we are giving Craig David a run for his money. He didn't have a suicide attempt to add to the mix. Maybe we would chill on Sunday with any luck.

"Let's go away for the weekend," he says excitedly, "we can go anywhere you want."

"Really?" I ask him. "How about Devon? It's a bit of a drive but we'll stick our favourite tunes on, buy snacks, it will be fun if you think you're up to it that is."

"Sounds like a plan," he says, turning into Tigger once again and bouncing around.

We shower, get dressed and are on the road by 7:30. We stop at a petrol station and stock up on chocolate and fizzy drinks. Luckily, we don't have any kids to witness our bad eating habits or my dentist come to that. Joseph has his sunglasses on again and he is also wearing his new watch. He didn't want to put it on in case it got scratched, but I had told him not to be so stupid. At which point he had just smiled and done as he was told. We listen to all the familiar tunes on his playlist. I practically know them all off by heart, anyway. Coldplay features heavily and someone called Elbow. Not really my thing, but I would humour him for now being as he was technically still in recovery. We make good time and are nearing Devon by 10:30.

We still don't have any accommodation booked, so we will have to take our chances later. We are going to visit another National Trust property, Greenway, as I have a fascination with all things Agatha Christie, and he is being nice to me. It was her holiday home, which overlooks the River Dart. It featured in an episode of Poirot entitled 'Dead Man's Folly' and I am looking forward to soaking up the ambience of the place. I thought he might object, but he seems quite happy to let me have my own way. Definitely a keeper, this one. I think to myself. I don't think I could get rid of him now, even if I wanted to. He's running through my veins whether I like it or not.

We park up and walk towards the house. It turns out to be quite a long walk, as it happens. You can go by boat, but we opt to drive and then walk the rest of the way. It is a beautiful cream coloured character house in an elevated position overlooking the river. There are a few deck chairs strategically placed to take in the view. I can see why she spent so much time here writing. The views are magnificent. We opt to go on a tour of the house. It is full of quirky pieces as you would expect. I believe she was quite a character. The rooms all branch off of a central hallway. Some rooms are blocked off with rope, but there is still plenty to see. We head upstairs and tour the bedrooms and finally a study. Copies of her books adorn the shelves. I pause for a while and take in the atmosphere of the room. I imagine her clicking away on her typewriter writing about the little Belgian and his grey cells and how they are working. I imagine Poirot saying one of my favourite lines, 'You have, how they say, a skeleton in the armour?' The thought tickles me. It appears that Joseph is enjoying it almost as much as me.

We leave and take a walk down to the boathouse. It is a quaint looking wooden building overlooking the river. The sun dances as it skims the water and little sail boats bob up and down all by themselves. Even on an autumn day it shines like a polished jewel. We meander back up through all the specimen plants and trees and beyond to the restaurant where we enjoy yet another cream tea. I'm glad to have seen it with him it has made it all the more special. We walk and talk as we make our way back to the waiting Porsche and drive off in search of accommodation.

As we fly along the country road, I look across and notice

there is a little station with a steam train waiting next to it. For a second I imagine it to be the Orient Express waiting to take us on an exciting journey to Istanbul. Maybe we will do that another time I hope so. He parks up and does a Google search on his phone and manages to book us a room at a hotel. A quaint little place overlooking the sea according to trip adviser.

We arrive at the room to settle in and I make a point of hanging everything up and clearing the bed of debris. We run a bath and fill it with an assortment from the array of goodies we find in the bathroom. The bubbles are about a metre high by the time we have finished mixing them like lotions and potions. We lol around in the bath for a while, then make our way to the bedroom.

"Let's try something different this time" he says grinning. He places me down on a chair and parts my legs.

"Didn't we do this last week or was it just me?" I say laughing.

"Oh yes, he says I'd forgotten about that."

"Not that I'm complaining," I tell him.

I am frightened he will change his mind and stop. He spends a long time attending to my needs. My gratefulness can be measured by the blotches sited on my neck and chest. We are running out of new things to try, but the old ones have now become like old master's, each one a classic in their own right.

Everything seems to run like clockwork. Optimal satisfaction is always guaranteed. I return the favour and then we fall onto the bed and sleep for a while. We lie there once again, comfortable in each-other's company.

When we wake up it is dark outside, so we get ourselves dressed up and head off to a local restaurant.

"I have a surprise for you."

"What is it?" I say excitedly, sounding like a kid opening a present at Christmas.

"Later" he says mysteriously.

I have on another of my little black dresses. My hair is in an updo with cascading curls at the side. He has opted for the smart casual approach. Dark blue trousers and a light blue shirt. His eyes were now returning to their usual sexiness. His watch is still looking fresh out of the box and provided just a little dash of bling. We are sat inside overlooking the sea.

"This is lovely." I say to him.

"Was this my surprise?" I ask. We can't really see much

outside it's too dark.

"Yes, you said you liked Mexican food, so I thought I'd bring you to a Mexican restaurant."

I try not to look too disappointed.

"Great, thanks," I say, smiling at him. I thought he had something important to tell me. We decide to order lots of different dishes and put them in the middle of the table and allow ourselves to just dig in. A multitude of dips and nachos with cheese, fajitas, spicy rice and a few other little side dishes.

Someone at another table has a birthday today, so their family are singing Happy Birthday to them as they blow out the candles on a cake. There is a good atmosphere with lots of chatter going on all around us. Our food arrives at last and we get stuck into it. I have allowed just enough room for churros and chocolate sauce. We are treated to another round of Happy Birthday from another corner of the restaurant.

"There are a lot of celebrations going on in here tonight," I say to him.

"Yes. It seems to be celebration central," he says shouting to be heard above the noise.

When the dessert arrives, I sit back and watch him dipping churros in chocolate sauce and then slowly and seductively licking it off. I know exactly what he is trying to do to me, and it's not going to work. I deliberately avert my gaze when I feel him looking at me.

"It's been a perfect day today." I say, feeling completely happy once again.

"Why don't we order champagne, Jess? Everyone else is celebrating, why not us?"

"Ok good idea," I tell him, "you order the champagne, I need to pop to the ladies to powder my nose." Really, it was to get the chocolate sauce off my face as I can feel it starting to set.

When I return to the table Joseph is on the phone. It had better not be 'you know who' I think to myself. It is Celine as it turns out asking him about something. I just hear him say "I'll let you know later".

"Hi Mum!" I shout towards the phone as I know this will make her smile. She is talking in such a loud voice that I feel as if she is stood right next to me.

She laughs and shouts "Hi" back to me.

When Joseph has ended the call I ask, "Is everything ok?"

"Fine," he says, "she just wondered how we are. I was telling her all about today. She wishes she was here with us. I think she gets a bit bored with my dad sometimes."

I hadn't noticed the champagne on the table.

Everyone gets up and dashes outside. Apparently, they are having a firework display on the beach which means we will be exchanging singing and shouting for whoops and bangs closely followed by an ooh and an ah. We are the only ones left in the restaurant now, even the waiters have gone outside onto the balcony for a closer look.

"Drink up." he says looking at my drink.

"Are you trying to get me drunk?"

"Something like that," he says grinning, "Hold on," he says as I put the glass up to my mouth. "There is something lying in the bottom."

"What is it," I panic, "It's not a worm out of a tequila bottle, is it?"

I look into the bottom of the glass to see something sparkly shining back at me. I put my fingers in the glass and pull it out. It is the biggest diamond ring I have ever seen.

He says, "Pass it to me a second." I hand it to him. He takes it from me and places it on my engagement finger.

"There," he says, "that's better. It is with its rightful owner now."

With tears of joy, I lean forward and kiss him on the mouth. Once I cry, I can't stop. Soon we are both laughing and crying at the same time.

"Is this what you had hidden in the drawer?" I say, putting two and two together.

"It might have been," he says casually. "I've known you were the one for a while, I just wasn't ready to tell you yet."

"How long have you known?" I ask.

"Since the first moment I saw you."

"About as long as me then," I say, beaming at him.

We both grin at each-other. In fact, we can't stop smiling. We pay the bill and go back to the car. I can't stop looking at my finger. It fits perfectly.

"How did you know my size?"

"You left a jewellery box out in the bedroom. I removed one ring and measured it. Mum has one of those old-fashioned ring gauges in her drawer of curiosities in the kitchen."

"What is that?" I ask him.

"It's the one drawer that has everything in it they don't

know what to do with."

"Oh," I say, "I think we all have one of those, I know I do."

"Anyway, I made a note of the size and I bought the ring in Selfridges on Monday at the same time I bought the bracelet. I slipped it into my pocket before you saw it, and I was just waiting for the right moment. Now seems like the right time. Mum was ringing to see if I had asked you yet."

"So, she knew all about it."

"She found it the other day when…" and he stops, "I had left the box on the table next to the bed. I had been looking at it and trying to work out what to do to put things right. Anyway, as they say, the rest is history. Thank god."

"When do you want to get married?" I ask him. "Next year or the year after?"

"I thought we had already decided. Christmas Eve, wasn't it?"

"Can we plan and organise a wedding in eight weeks?"

"Well, Mum has a friend who knows the vicar of St Anne's. They have had a cancellation. Christmas Eve is available if we want it."

"Ok. We are doing this," I say, still in a state of disbelief.

"You haven't even met my family yet. They are going to be surprised to say the least."

"Not a problem, is it?"

"I know they will love you just as much as I do. How could they not love that face?"

He is putting on his best puppy dog eyes. "Alan will be shocked, won't he?"

"Maybe not as shocked as you might think."

"You mean he knows already?"

"I sent him a text earlier when we were back at the hotel, while I was waiting for you to get ready. He is really pleased for us. He thinks it's great."

"Is there anyone that doesn't know?"

"Not really,"

"Oh well, I say it saves me having to tell them I guess."

No Turning Back

Whehn I wake up the next morning, the first thing I do is to glance at my hand. It's the brightest, most beautiful ring I have ever seen. I hope he didn't spend too much. Then again, I had just bought him a very expensive watch, so I guess that makes us even. I grab a notebook and pen from my bag and begin to make notes. 'Things to do for the wedding.' God knows where we will get a caterer from at this short notice. I remember that Anton has a catering business on the side. It is yet another one of his side-lines. He would be sure to do it. So that is the catering, and the cake sorted. The church is sorted thanks to Celine. We will worry about the rest later.

Just then, Joseph wakes up and puts out his hand. I take it and place it against my cheek.

"How's my fiancé?" He enquires, looking pleased with himself.

"How do you think?" I say, giving him a smile. "If you had to hazard a guess?"

"Happy I hope, like me"

"You have your answer" I say kissing him on the mouth.

"Do you think we should invite David and Abbey to the

wedding?" he asks.

"That's your business and I'm not getting involved. I don't see why Abbey and the kids should be punished when they haven't done anything wrong."

"I can't face speaking to him at the moment, besides, I need to make him suffer a bit."

"What will happen at work?"

"He's keeping everything ticking over. He's not that stupid. He won't do anything that might jeopardise the future of the company. I think Mum gave him a right flee in his ear by all accounts. She seemed quite proud of it."

"Did she tell you what she said to him?"

"Told him to buzz off or something just as terrible, I expect," said Joseph.

I whisper to him the words she had told me she said to him.

"Christ," he said, "I didn't know she knew words like that."

"She's a real ledge, isn't she?" I say to him.

"You could say that," he says with a proud look on his face.

I am glad we are both on the same side, that is for sure. I felt, with Celine on our side, we could tackle anything.

We decide to shower, get dressed and head down to breakfast. The restaurant is fairly empty, so we are able to flirt opening without fear of putting people off their breakfasts. I still can't stop staring at my finger. It's strange, it's not as if I haven't been engaged before. Just not to him. I am wondering if I have got too used to his good looks now. perhaps, I will start to take them for granted.

But as he gives me that look from across the restaurant, I needn't have worried as my heart still jumps in my chest. I watch him as he returns to the table.

"What is it?" he says inquisitively.

How can I explain how I feel about him when even I don't comprehend or fully understand my feelings? He completes me, that's all there is to it.

We finish our breakfast and head to the beach. It is looking pretty deserted as we walk along hand-in-hand. Just a couple of dog walkers for company. The dog is the only one foolish enough to jump in and out of the freezing cold water. We spot a bench and sit down. You'd think we would be all benched out by now.

"You won't go off me, will you?" I say to him, feeling worried.

"What sort of silly question is that?" He says putting his arm around me.

"Andrew did," I say, this time sounding upset.

"He was soft in the head if you ask me." He says in his best irritated voice.

"You have got a point!" I say looking at him and laughing. I can picture us in our old age making love in the garden. Me sitting in a chair with my legs apart. When suddenly my knees lock and he will attempt to carry me back to the house still stuck in that position. We have a while before that will happen so I won't think about it, I will just enjoy the moment.

We are already beginning to finish one another's sentences. I ask him, "Do you think that's normal?"

"That's nothing," he says, "my parents don't even have to speak now they just use telepathy instead. She knows exactly what he wants before he even asks for it."

"Do you think we could go to Paris sometime?" I ask.

"I'd love to take you to Paris."

"Not yet but soon."

I have visions of us rolling around between the sheets and feeding one another croissants and Pain au Chocolat. When we have absolutely no choice but to leave the room, we will stroll around Paris along the Seine watching pavement artists as they paint. We will visit the Louvre and marvel at the Mona Lisa and Monet paintings before visiting the Notre Dame Cathedral and light a candle. We will have lunch in a pretty little bistro in a side street and grab lavender macaroon's in a nearby patisserie which you would later feed me in bed as if they are lilac sugar covered kisses that dissipate on my lips.

"That sound's perfect. Let's get a flight, we can be there this afternoon."

"I can't, I've got to work tomorrow, remember?"

"Oh damn, I'd forgotten about that. I don't want you to go." He says pulling his wounded look out of the bag.

"I don't want to either, but its only for a few hours and you can pick me up and take me for lunch if you like. Maybe you could pop in and speak to Alan at the same time. Just long enough to rub Hazels nose in it. I give you permission to be all over me like a rash."

"I think I can manage that," he says, sexily kissing me on the mouth.

We pack up the car and head back to Surrey. Joseph actually allows me to select my music to play. By now, even he is bored of his endless Coldplay collection as great as it is. I play Attention by Charlie Puth. Yet another of my personal favourites. I seem to have more favourites than the late Bruce Forsyth. We sing along, pausing and sighing in the same part of the song as Charlie before belting out the final chorus.

"I've never seen your hair out of place, it's looking a bit tousled, darling." I say, teasing him.

He looks over his sunglasses and says, "is tousled good?", not really sure what that means.

"Anything looks good on you," I say, smiling at him. "Besides, I shall sort you out in the shower later if you like. Your hair, that is."

He closes his mouth again and concentrates on his driving. We pull into the familiar drive to see Abbey sat outside.

"I've been dreading this moment."

Joseph decides to take charge and heads over to her for a chat. I watch as they talk and finally; he hugs her, and she starts to cry. They walk over to me and she runs up to me and hugs me tightly.

"I'm so sorry," she says, "David told me everything, eventually. I had to force it out of him, much to his embarrassment. Needless to say, he is sleeping in the spare room at the moment. I need to think about what I am going to do and consider my options."

"Come in and spend time with us," I say to her, trying to cheer her up a bit.

"Neither of us blame you for this. I'm still glad to have met you. It's just your husband I'm not a big fan of."

"Me neither," she says apologetically.

"Joseph will sort it all out. They still have to work together after all. Unless David is planning on handing in his notice, that is?"

"He doesn't want to," says Abbey.

"Well, that is for Joseph and David to sort out. Not us."

I make a pot of tea and sandwiches. We sit at the table while I tell Abbey all about our weekend. She spots the big diamond on my finger and nudges me.

"Is that what I think it is?"

"Yep" I say grinning like a Cheshire cat.

"At least something positive has come out of this week then. When is the wedding?" Abbey asks.

"In about eight weeks' time. Christmas eve. The vicar had a cancellation, so we are hoping we have just enough time to organise everything. Maybe you can help me with that if you want to?"

She starts to cry again, "I'd love to. Thank you."

I tell her I would like Clara and Bluebell to be bridesmaids. You'd think I had just told her she had won the lottery.

"I can't wait to tell them. They will be so excited."

"Who is going to be best-man Joseph?" Abbey asks.

"I was hoping if I ever tied the knot it would be David stood next to me but, under the circumstances, Ab's I'm just not sure he's up to the job. I will have to meet up with him and thrash everything out for all our sakes."

"Your mum gave him a real kicking by all accounts. I can't say I blame her. You and your mum are so close. There was no way she was going to let him off the hook that easily."

We get things back to normality by chatting about the girls and what they've been doing at school.

"We will have to have one of those girly nights," she says to me. "Paw over lots of those glossy Bridle magazines whilst drinking copious amounts of alcohol. What do you say?"

"Sounds good to me. Sooner rather than later, though. I need to get things moving."

"This week then?" She says excitedly.

I nod and smile. "I can invite a couple of friends from work as well." I say to her. "We can all stay at my place and have a pyjama party."

"You don't wear any!" Joseph says smiling.

"No," I say, "because you keep ripping them off me."

"Guilty as charged" he says holding his hands up.

"Not that I'm complaining!" I say, kissing him and stroking his face.

Abbey makes her excuses and heads for the door. We say goodbye and each give her a big hug and tell her not to worry as everything will sort it's self out. She sighs and gives us a smile as she gets in her car and drives away. We go back inside, take one look at the washing up and then each-other.

"Let's just go to bed" I say.

"I am tired," says Joseph.

"I'm not tired," I say, "Far from it!"

"I like your way of thinking," he says, running up the stairs.

"What have I told you about running on the stairs?" I shout up at him.

"Bath or shower?" he shouts at me from the bathroom.

"Either" I tell him, "you choose."

"Shower" he says stripping off and jumping in.

I get undressed and follow him. We hug and kiss for a couple of minutes before my head disappears between his legs. He holds on to my head while I suck on his. The water is cascading down my face and into my eyes, but I keep going until he is completely satisfied.

"Where did you learn to do that?" he says.

"The school of hard cocks? I mean knocks!" I say, laughing hysterically.

He just shakes his head at, yet another of, my failed attempts at humour. We get out of the shower and dry ourselves off. He chases me into the bedroom and places me face down onto the bed. This time he catches me before I bounce to the floor. He gently massages my back and shoulders, then moves down to my lower half. He massages my buttocks and calves before turning me over and massaging me with his tongue. By the time he has finished, I am completely spent. I just lie for a few minutes enjoying the sense of calmness he has instilled in me, which has started at my feet and is working its way up my body. He joins me again and lies next to me with his head on my chest.

"Everything is going to be alright," he says, "I don't want you to worry about a thing." He senses I am still apprehensive about David.

"I know it is. I know I can trust you to make it right. You make everything alright. Just a word from you makes all my worries melt away."

He just smiles and holds me tighter.

The Cinderella Moment

Next morning I'm up and ready by 7:45.

"Don't forget your supposed to be driving me to work."

"Oh sorry, I forgot." He says throwing on his clothes and cleaning his teeth. We grab tea and toast and head out of the door. He takes the Porsche as he wants to give Nigel a clean before lunch, not that he needs it. But men love washing cars, that much I have learnt. He drops me a little way away so it will be a big surprise when he turns up later. I keep my engagement ring out of sight just for the moment. When I walk in the office Hazel is there with another one of my work colleagues.

"Have you had a pleasant week?" they both ask me.

"Not really," I say, trying to sound miserable, "I had to spend the week in bed."

"Oh, no," they say, "That's awful. Sod's law is if you have a week off you usually go down with something." They tell me. Or down on something, I think to myself.

But just say, "I know. Just my luck."

"How's lover boy?" Hazel says, smiling.

"If you mean Joseph Mathews, you will have to ask him yourself. I'm sure he's fine." I say in a couldn't care less manner. They take this to mean I haven't seen him since Friday. I smile as I walk out of the office with my back to them. The morning passes by slowly but it is now 11:25. Joseph is supposed to be seeing Alan for a quick chat before we leave at 12:00. This time I definitely hear him before I see him as Nigel roars into the car park. A beautiful vision in blue and chrome.

A few people move across to the window to see what all the fuss is about. He climbs out of the car wearing a white shirt, dark blue trousers and a blue Ralph Lauren sweater. He is wearing the watch I bought him. It is rapidly becoming a regular fixture on his wrist.

"He's too smooth for my liking." Robert says eying him through the upstairs window.

"I know what you mean," I say, nodding in agreement and trying to catch my breath, "the guy does love himself." The mere sight of him sending my body into overdrive. I wonder what he will say and do, and I just hope he doesn't do anything too embarrassing. When he makes his entrance, he blanks me and walks straight into Alans office.

"I told you I didn't know how he was." I tell a surprised

but pleased Hazel.

"I thought you were joking." she says, almost feeling sorry for me. I busy myself with filing away paperwork while he chats to Alan. I go to walk downstairs and collect my bag.

Alan says, "Where do you think you're going?"

"Toilet" I say pretending to look confused. Joseph and Alan come out of his office carrying a bottle of champagne.

"I have an announcement to make."

"What now?" Hazel says under her breath, "I want my lunch sometime today." she says muttering again.

"Joseph and Jess are getting married." By this time, I have taken my diamond sparkler and placed it proudly on my finger. Hazels face is a picture. She practically has 'What the F…!' tattooed on her forehead. There is a silence quickly followed by a cheer and applause. Robert doesn't look happy, but that was to be expected, I guess. He has been in love with me for years. He's a lovely guy, but just not right for me. Maybe he and Hazel should get together. Now there's a thought. I could do some matchmaking. My mind whirring yet again. Joseph walks over to me and puts his arms around me. Everyone says aw and I get really embarrassed.

"Come on, missis," he says, "let's go and eat."

We wave goodbye, letting Nigel have the final word as we fly out of the carpark and out of sight. I can only imagine the conversations that are now taking place back in the office.

"Didn't embarrass you, did I back there?" Joseph says, looking worried.

"God, no, the only reason I was embarrassed was because I don't deserve you. I can't believe out of all the women in the world you want me. You could have your pick."

"Yes, and I have, and I've picked you. For your information, I couldn't be happier and don't you forget it".

We enjoy a leisurely lunch at a local pub. He tucks into possibly the biggest burger I have ever seen. Complete with cheese, crispy bacon, and fries. I have a rather predictable lasagne and salad. I make it my mission in life to taste test all the lasagnes in the local area and rate them afterwards just for my own benefit. We talk about the wedding arrangements or lack of. As he is still on light duties for the next few days, I will give him a list of jobs to do. Anton has already agreed to do the catering and cake, which is great. I have made a few phone calls about flowers, so that is underway as well. We have a few meetings with the vicar to look forward to, just to select hymns and bits and pieces. We are going ahead with my marquis idea, and Joseph is looking into that. Celine is positively beside herself and is already shopping for hats. I have told my family, who were shocked but pleased and are all looking forward to it. Lots of things are starting to get ticked off the list, thank goodness. Just suits, bride-maid dresses, my dress, rings, invitations, honeymoon.

"Just let me handle it." he says "Don't you worry about anything. We'll have another crack at it tomorrow. Mum can help me. She is itching to get involved. My dad is just glad of the distraction. It means he can go off with his golf buddies anytime he wants."

When I get back to the office Hazel is still sat at her desk holding her head. Unable to comprehend what has just happened.

"Who does that happen to?" she says staring at me. I put my finger up to my lips.

"It's come to me," Hazel says "Cinder-bleeding-rella!"

Dotting the 'I's

O ver the coming week, or so, we manage to cross the majority of items off the to-do list. Celine, Abbey, and I decide to have a girly morning shopping for dresses. We start with mine first; of course. I want to get it out of the way so I can relax a bit. They both cry when I emerge from the changing room.

"I hope they are happy tears," I confess. Before doing a 360 in the mirror and asking them, "Do you think my bum looks big in this?"

"Yes" Abbey say's. "Joseph will love it." I mess around running my hand over my curves and saying "They don't call me Jessica rabbit for nothing" before pouting and winking at them.

Abbey says, "I think you'd give Kim K a run for her money in that dress."

I shoot them a worried look.

"We are winding you up. It hugs you in all the right places, that's all," Abbey says smiling. "He won't be able to keep his eyes to himself."

Good, because those baby blues are all mine. They are like

a midnight sky on a clear evening. Complete with stars that wink at you. A beautiful dark inky blue. A deeper shade of blue.

"She's thinking about him again." Abbey says, knowing me too well.

"Good," Celine says, "I think it's wonderful."

She pulls out a tissue to wipe her eyes, which then makes me cry, which then makes Abbey cry. A kind of domino effect, you could say.

We are crying wrecks by the time we leave the shop, having picked out a pair of pretty strappy shoes to match the dress. Celine is lending me a necklace that belonged to her mother, Elouise. The shop assistant has convinced me to go for a pair of white gloves and a cape type thing with a hood. I worry I will look like a boxer entering the ring. I shall have to add the rocky theme to the list of hymns that should perk things up a bit. I imagine Doreen the organist is always belting that out of a Sunday morning.

We make our way to the vintage tea shop opposite. I am treating us all to an afternoon tea. It is not long before we are seated at a table, tucking into a huge tiered cake stand filled with sandwiches and every yummy cake you can imagine. Mis-matched teapot and teacups adorn the table. I feel like

Alice in Wonderland. All that is missing is my Mad Hatter. Even when I am not with him, he is all I can think about.

Joseph sends me a text to say, 'He hopes we are having a good time and that he is missing me.' He tries to wind me up by telling me he has decided not to bother with clothes today and is lying on the bed with something in his hand thinking of me. I text him back and say, 'I know exactly where you are. You are out with your dad. Celine has already told me. A pint and burger at the pub.' 'Well,' he replies, 'I am sat with a large piece of meat in front of me. It's just this time it's encased in a brioche bun.' 'Thanks for putting that thought in my head when I am trying to make sensible conversation with your mother.' He will be roaring with laughter now; I just know it. Passing it off as a funny video he has just watched on You Tube to his dad.

We seem to have put the sex part of our relationship on the back burner. Exchanging make love for making lists. We climb into bed at night and just make hundreds of lists for no apparent reason, which usually make no sense when we read them in the morning. I thought the wedding preparations might have been too much for him, but he seems to take it all in his stride. He has been for a few counselling sessions and it seems to have helped a lot.

Joseph and David thrashed out their differences the other night over a few beers. They seem to be getting things back on track. I on the other hand am staying as far away from David as possible whilst remaining civil. It is going to take a long time before I can learn to trust him again. He and Abbey on the other hand appear to be slowing piecing their marriage back together, mainly for the sake of the children, but I know she still loves him and him, her.

Alan has been great and has given me time off for fittings and appointments, which has been a great help. My family are still yet to meet Joseph, although we have had a few Zoom calls, so at least they feel as though they know him a bit. My two brothers are a lot older than me and live several hours' drive away, so I don't see them much, anyway. My parents have retired to Spain. Although not wealthy, they had made a lot of lucky investments along the way so, in due course, this had allowed them to purchase a small house with a swimming pool. More of a bath really, but it keeps them happy. As soon as I was firmly settled in my own house, they took to calling me less and less. They are far too busy sunning themselves and throwing themselves whole heartedly into their retirement. I guess they have worked hard I shouldn't begrudge them a bit of happiness.

There will just be a few friends and close family at the

wedding. I guess that takes the pressure off a bit. A select crowd, but we didn't care. As long as he was stood next to me, I couldn't care less, and I knew it was the same for him. We would rather have a real blow out on the honeymoon, anyway. Make it an event to remember. Although, trying for Joe Junior would do that all by itself. I can't wait to give him the son he so desires. It will be like giving him his watch all over again, only two hundred million times better.

Joseph has returned to work part time and on the other days he takes it easy and just does bits and pieces as required. The frantic phone-calls from David are becoming a thing of the past. I wonder if Joseph has asked David to be his best man. I don't want to know the answer, so I don't ask the question. I will just wait for the big reveal on Christmas Eve along with everybody else. Work is keeping me occupied. Hazel, having now got over her initial shock, is seemingly pleased for me. I feel excited as the invitations have just arrived back from the printers.

Miss Jessica Stanning

and Mr Joseph Matthews

are tying the knot and would like to invite

....

To celebrate their wedding day on

Saturday 24th December

at St Anne's church

at 12.30pm

and afterwards at Hidcote House

Please R.S.V.P. by 18th December

…to freeze your arse off in a marquis.

We've left that bit out. Although we could probably all fit around Celine and Johns kitchen table if push came to shove or if we have two feet of snow which is possible but unlikely.

At least we don't have a wedding planner like the one in 'Father of the Bride' another one of my personal favourites dusted off and wheeled out every Christmas. Swan ice sculptures! I grimace at the thought. I laugh at the thought of a 'Franck' to contend with. Then I realise I just have Joseph

Francis, John Francis and my dad Francis James instead. To be totally frank, I wasn't looking forward to it. I tease Joseph in bed that evening.

"Only two hours and twenty-seven days until I can start my illicit affair with Anton, the wife stealer."

He glares at me through narrowed eyes.

"Don't get upset," I say stroking his face. "I'm only joking. Besides, that started months ago." I say rolling about on the bed laughing.

Just then I feel a pillow clonk me on the back of the head.

"If you keep winding me up like that, I'm going to have to keep asking you 'Hey, how you doin?' just to annoy you."

"If you do that, I am going to have to start calling you Joey. How about that?"

He thinks for a moment. "When you say it, it doesn't sound that bad. You make everything sound dirty with that deep sexy voice of yours," he tells me.

"That's rich coming from you. With your buttery, sexy, let me take you to bed and read you a story vernacular."

"Sounds impressive," he says nodding and looking pleased with himself.

"It is," I say, smiling at him. "I always get a flash of excitement when I see your name pop up on my phone. Even if you are just calling to tell me you've picked up milk from the petrol station. I imagine it to be the creamiest, most sumptuous milk I have ever tasted. Freshly squeezed from the cow that morning."

"Allow me to tell you a story," he says, taking away my notebook and putting it down on the table next to him. "Once upon a time, there was handsome prince. But he had a very big problem, and he didn't know what to do about it."

He then grabs my hand and places it so I can feel the size of him.

"But then, I do know it's going to have a very happy ending." he says grabbing my face in his hands.

We turn out the lights and let the story unfold before coming to a dramatic conclusion all of our own.

We have now reached the beginning of December. This I know because Starbucks have just started selling mince pies again. We have bought one another a chocolate advent calendar so we can tick off the day's till the big day in chocolate. I have red Lindt balls in mine, and I have selected larger chocolates for Joseph so I can fulfil my chocolate fantasy as I watch him lick and devour each one; and that's before breakfast... This usually gave me a moment of bliss. If a twitch can ever be described as blissful? It leaves me considering if I have a chocolate fetish that I need to discuss with somebody. Maybe just a Joseph sized fetish that is more likely.

"Don't forget," I shout to him as he's walking out of the door. "You promised you'd pick up the rings and the girl's necklaces."

"I won't forget," he says, running back to kiss me goodbye.

I give him a look and he just stare's back at me and says, "We haven't got time." I give him an upset face. He laughs and hurries out of the door. He pretends to have forgotten something and comes back inside. He then gently pushes me against the wall and kisses me passionately on the lips. "You are going to get me sacked!" He says pretending to be angry.

"They can't sack you, you're the boss." I watch Joseph as he jumps into the car and drives off, leaving a wake of gravel behind him. I hope he gets home early tonight, or I shall have to install the traffic light system I had threatened to use. It had not been required up until now. But I think the time has come so I could give it a whirl this evening just for a laugh. I want to see how quickly he can get back from work when he needs to.

My thoughts return to the wedding. We have ordered unicorn necklaces for the two girls to match their bracelets. They have pretty sugary pink dresses with fluffy bolero jackets to keep them warm. When asked to choose shoes, they both selected furry boots, much to Abbey's dismay. But I have decided I will just run with it. You can hardly see the boots under their long dresses anyhow. I have decided on a white, pink and lilac theme. Pretty roses with little sprigs of dried lavender adorning them. All rustically tied with a pretty ribbon. As lavender is out of season dried will just have to do. I will have to spray it with lavender oil or something. That should have us tearing up in the church, that's for sure.

The men will have a miniature version adorning their buttonholes. At last, I will be able to fulfil my top hat fantasy. That's exactly what I want to see as I poke my head around the bedroom door on our wedding night. I got him to dress up as a unicorn. Maybe a mad hatter isn't out of the question. I laugh out loud. Everyone in the office knows me so well by now that they choose to just ignore me and carry-on working. In the beginning they would question me and say "What are you laughing at?" now they don't bother. I hardly know myself most of the time, anyway. A funny comment someone has made earlier in the day can have me in a fit of giggles. What

I did know was that I was developing ruddy great laughter lines, which is something I will need to address.

"She's at it again." Hazel says, rolling her eyes. "She's probably imagining him dressed up as the Milk Tray Man and climbing in her window to give her a nice big present!"

"Joseph in a top hat." I say, but I reprimand myself for not thinking of the Milk Tray thing myself. I just need him to pick up a box of chocolates on his way home. Maybe the petrol station will have a selection, but a balaclava? We'd just have to improvise. Maybe a sleep mask. I had a black one of those kicking around from our fifty shades evening. I put on the blindfold while he placed yummy things into my mouth. You get the picture. I do like the sound of it, though. He could peel it off to reveal his beautiful blue eyes. Climbing up the drainpipe could be a problem in a blindfold. I can see why the balaclava might be essential to the operation. Instigating the traffic light system and carrying out my current fantasy all in one night might be a bit much, even for him. After all, he wasn't superman. "Shit!" I shout out again, letting my imagination run riot. I would have to give up thinking. I would have to send him a text telling him to get home now and, oh by the way, can you be dressed as the Milk Tray Man. Don't bother with your keys because I want you to shin up the drainpipe. The mad thing is I think he would do it, but I would just have to place that one on the backburner for later.

It will keep for another time.

The Run Up

It is now just three weeks until the wedding. Party season is in full swing already. Joseph and I have become like the proverbial ships passing in the night. He always seems to be out wining-and-dining with customers and clients. I miss having him all to myself like I did in the beginning of our relationship. I busy myself with the wedding arrangements and when Saturday finally arrives, we both heave a massive sigh of relief. I wake up to feel a hand moving between my legs.

"Are you trying to tell me something?" I say sarcastically.

"We haven't seen one another that much lately. I miss you," he says with his sad face.

"I miss you too," I say, staring into his eyes lovingly.

We have a bath together, which ends up in a water fight. I try to jump out of the bath quickly and nearly do the splits on the tiled floor. He catches me and leads me onto the floor, which is now adorned with a vast pile of towels. "How much mess do you think one woman can make"? I ask, laughing.

"I want you to feel as though you are floating on a fluffy cloud."

"Aw lovely." I say, trying to empty my thoughts. I want nothing to take my mind off the pleasurable experience. His tongue sends tiny shocks through my body with every probing stroke. Till I can't suppress it any longer.

"Still got it, never lost it!" he says modestly whilst checking himself out in the bathroom mirror.

"And so modest to boot." I say laughing to myself. He picks me up in his arms and slams me down on the countertop by mistake. "You don't have to treat me like china," I say sarcastically "I won't break.".

"Sorry," he says, "you slipped out of my arms."

What he did next needed no apology. You'd think his life depended on it. He makes quiet moaning noises as he moves back and forth in tune with my body. When he has finished, I climb down, have a quick shower and walk towards the bedroom still holding my bottom form where he has thrown me onto the counter.

"Sorry, want me to kiss it better for you?"

"No, just be gentler next time."

"Okay" he says, covering my bottom with kisses, anyway.

"You ought to wear a wrestling outfit whilst jumping from the chest of drawers. What would your wrestling name be?" I ask curiously, "How about the blue-eyed assassin?" I say to him.

"I know what yours would be. Two tonne Jess."

He only gets away with this comment because I am 5ft 3 and of slight build. We grab breakfast and go into London on a Christmas shopping spree. We aren't sure when we will next be able to do it as the wedding is taking up so much of our time.

We head out to nearby Woking and jump on a fast train into Waterloo. We get the tube to Oxford Street along with every other living sole. We head to Liberty first, where we buy all sorts of goodies for Celine. A scarf, a pretty diamond brooch that looks like a sprig of lavender, perfume, chocolates and various scented lotions and potions. I will buy a basket and make it look nice when I get home. Joseph disappears to find things for his dad, freeing me up to have fun upstairs in the Christmas department. I buy various pretty baubles and hanging ornaments in every colour of the rainbow. When they are bagged up, I head to the cushion department just in case. A girl can never have too many cushions. Sure enough, I spy another couple to add to the collection at home. I head back downstairs to find Joseph carrying his dad's presents. He looks worried when he sees the size of my bags. I have bought a multitude of tree decorations.

"You didn't seem to have any." I say in my defence.

"That's probably because I don't."

"I want everything to be perfect this year." I tell him.

"It will be, I've got you." he says kissing me.

The shop assistant looks like she is going to be sick but just smiles and says, "Bless."

I put the bags down for a second and pretend to look at my phone. He picks them all up and heads out onto the street. Mission accomplished, I think, smiling to myself. It never fails that one. You could say it's got Christmas bells on it. We head to Selfridges, passing a sea of yellow bags going in the opposite direction. Their owners clutching them tightly as they are full of precious Christmas cargo. We have fun in the toy department choosing items for Clara and Bluebell and cute paper to wrap them in. We buy a few gifts for David and Abbey. Although every time I see David, I can still only picture the stereotypical pantomime villain. As I climb the escalator, I hope I don't hear 'Last Christmas' playing. It evoked unhappy memories of a Christmas past. Instead, a predictable Mariah Carey is telling us what she wants for Christmas. I find a few small gifts for my family as we don't really buy for each other.

"Is there anything you want?" he asks me.

I don't know why men do that. I'm never quite sure what I am supposed to say. It always seems like a loaded question somehow. I just say, "You with a big ribbon tied around your... waist."

"That's easy then." he says walking off the tech department. I follow and decide to ask him the same question. "A son." he answers casually.

I say, "No pressure there then?"

He say's "You did ask".

"Yes, I did?" The enormity of the task now weighing down on me. I just hope I can give him what he wants. You never know if you can conceive until you start trying. We still have time, but how much is anyone's guess.

We now have only two weeks to go. I decide today is the day to purchase our first Christmas tree. I head out to the garden centre with Celine in tow. We have a lovely time drinking tea and eating luxury mince pies adorned with a generous helping of clotted cream. Michael Bublé is playing in the background, telling us to have ourselves a merry little Christmas.

"To be honest, he wouldn't have to tell me twice," I say out loud.

"Good god no. I wouldn't mind finding him at the end of the bed on Christmas day in his little red hat and nothing else." Celine quickly responds.

"You go, girl!" I say encouragingly. She is quickly developing my sense of humour; I am proud to say. I was slowly infiltrating them one by one there was only John left and he was anyone's for a cherry pie so that would be easy.

"If the boys could hear us now, eh?" she says, laughing loudly.

"Joseph has probably got the place bugged." I say to her with a serious look on my face. "In case I'm having a secret rendezvous with Anton."

"Yes, he does get his knickers into a twist rather," says Celine supportively.

"I only have to go in the bakery and talk to him about lemon drizzle and macaroons and Joseph thinks it's a euphemism for something naughty and that we're speaking in some code or other. Did you get time to watch the Joe Wickes video I recommended to you? To help with your bad back." I ask Celine.

"It certainly gave me a good work out. I had to blow a few cobwebs off first, mind you, and after all, it has been a long time." I interpret the smile on her face and roar with laughter. It's not just John that can tune into her telepathic thoughts.

"Do you know what I say, Celine? A Joe Wicks a-day keeps the doctor away. You can keep your apples." I am proud she has come such a long way in such a short space of time.

"Going back to Joseph he just can't believe his luck Jess, that's all. He keeps waiting for something to go wrong."

"Nothing is going to go wrong," I say reassuringly "I will not let it. Not on my watch"

Let it Snow

The next morning the Christmas tree arrives. I underestimated how large it would be once the net was removed. Joseph arrives downstairs to see what can only be described as the goliath of the Christmas tree world. It is bending slightly at the top, so he has to help me take a bit off the top of it. Once in place, I add all the baubles and decorations I had bought in Liberty. I stand back to admire my handy work.

"Not bad, even if I do say so myself." I say admiringly.

"Less about me and more about the tree," he says, yet again blowing his own trumpet. He puts his arms around me from behind. "It does look lovely. Thank you for doing this. Sorry for being such a scrooge."

He hadn't really wanted to bother, but I had convinced him it was completely necessary. I added a few more accessories here and there, which I had gathered up from home to complete the look. I am very pleased with my efforts and have a congratulatory mug of tea and a fondant fancy.

We decide to have lunch in the pub and then take the dogs for a walk. We take our time getting ready and then do the short walk down to one of the village pubs. I decide to have a small glass of wine.

"I hope we don't end up in a ditch this afternoon."

"In your case," he says, "I'm sure it wouldn't be the first time."

"You cheeky so and so" and I pretend to swot him with my hand. He was of course correct in his assumption. Andrew and I used to do a lot of pub-crawls a few years back. That was the problem with being surrounded on all sides by pubs, I guess.

We eat our main course and order dessert. I tuck into my Lotus Biscoff cheesecake, making moaning noises all the while.

"What has that cheesecake got I haven't?"

"Nothing," I say, trying to make him feel better, "have you seen me cry yet?" I ask him.

"That was very endearing when you did that." he says teasing me.

"What do you mean," I say, "I do it most times."

"I guess I've just got used to it. Being fantastic. Par for the course, isn't it?"

"Am I just another one of your satisfied customers?" I ask

him, smiling.

"I always seem to score well on the satisfaction survey you fill out at the end."

"So does this cheesecake." I say making exaggerated pleasure noises. "You can't be jealous of a cheesecake." I say screaming with laughter. He picks up one of his profiteroles and rolls his tongue around it.

"Not nice is it?" he says pulling a face.

"I don't know, I'd say it's giving me a tingle." We pay the bill and start walking back to the house.

"Shall we not bother taking the dogs for a walk?"

"But they are really looking forward to it," I say, sounding disappointed.

"I'm looking forward to something else now." he says, grabbing hold of me.

"Can't we do both?" I say to him.

I see him digesting what I have just said. Take the dogs for a walk, then have some fun of our own.

"I guess so."

We rush back to the house and go get the dogs. Eric and Ernie are pleased to see us as we haven't seen them for ages.

Eric keeps jumping for a cuddle. So, I kiss him on the head and make a fuss of him.

Joseph just looks at me and say's "First the cheesecake, now him, when do I get my turn?"

"Good things come to those who wait." I tell him, patting him on the arm.

We make the short walk to the woods. Once we are there, we thoroughly enjoy ourselves. The dogs are in their element, sniffing everything like they are trying to track the scent of a small animal. They busy themselves, cocking their legs constantly and running through every muddy puddle they can find.

"I'm glad we didn't bring the car," he says, sounding relieved.

"I don't think your mum is going to be thrilled when she sees the gruesome twosome over there. Muddy and even muddier. You might have to hose them down first."

"And waste more valuable time?"

"Are we on a deadline I don't know about?" I ask him in an attempt to find out what the problem is.

"I'm just feeling a bit overwhelmed what with work and the wedding."

"I will make all your problems disappear when we get home. We are on the last stretch, not long now, and then we get to relax and enjoy ourselves."

"I know. I'm just over-reacting, that's all."

"At least you are talking to me, that's good."

We return to the house and Joseph gives the dogs a bath before taking them back to his mum and dad's. Meanwhile, I run a nice warm bath and climb in.

"I've lit the fire downstairs," he says with a glint in his eye "Perhaps we can have a roll around in front of it?"

"Sounds good." I say, giving him a smile.

I get out and dry myself off while he finishes bathing. I take my hair down and shake it out before spraying myself with Chanel. I put on a lacy thong and a pair of high-heeled shoes and make my way down to the living room. He is right behind me and slaps me on the bottom as I exaggerate my sexy strut. I reach the fire and stand still while he works his way down my body. He gently peels off my underwear, pulls me down towards him and I sit on top of him. I bend my knees and go up and down to maximum effect. Afterwards we lie in each-other's arms for a bit, just enjoying the moment.

"Are you feeling better now, Joseph?"

"Yes, I am."

"Well, that's good" I say as I smile up at him.

"I just want to spend as much time with you as possible. It's making me unhappy that I can't do that. I'm worried you will get fed up with me and leave."

"No, you are officially stuck with me now. You couldn't get rid of me if you tried". I say kissing his mouth and ruffling his hair. I see a weight visibly lift from his shoulders. He goes back to being happy Joseph again as we make our way upstairs to bed.

When I wake up in the morning, he is already nowhere to be seen. He has left me a note telling me he is missing me already. How can I be annoyed with him for not waking me up to say goodbye? I get ready for work and leave the house. I jump in my car and listen to life affirming music to cheer myself up. I feel better after a sing along and a jig about in the car.

We have now had all the invitations back and everyone that has been invited has said yes. I will have to try to fix up Hazel and Robert as they both deserve to be happy. But it seems my matchmaking skills will not be required on this occasion, as both of them seem to be very happy this morning. I sense something is afoot. Hazel is happily humming to herself as she sits at her desk, and this is not like her.

"Right," I say to her, "spill the beans." as soon as Robert disappears outside.

"Well," she says, moving closer and drawing me in. "Robert came over to mine for a drink on Friday and he never left. Seems as though this love bug of yours is catching."

I smile and say, "It's about time. I'm really pleased for you both. I was going to try to get you two together at the wedding."

"No need," she says, "I have taken control of the situation."

"You will have to give me all the gory details when you come round to the house at the end of the week."

"Great, I'm looking forward to it." I am having a bit of a hen doo. Just a couple of people over for a few drinks and nibbles. Maybe bust a few moves that sort of thing. Sit around in our pyjamas talking about men more like whilst drowning our sorrows. Except I don't feel like drowning my sorrows, for I am, quite possibly, the luckiest girl in the world. It is official.

The Hen Party

I don't know where this week has gone. It is Friday evening, and I am at my house waiting patiently for Hazel and Abbey to arrive. Joseph is going out for a drink with David, and I have managed to persuade John to go along to keep an eye on proceedings. When I open the door Hazel and Abbey are stood there already deep in conversation. They enter into the hallway and take themselves off on a private tour of the house. While they are gone, I pour out three glasses of wine and organise the nibbles in pretty bowls.

"So Hazel, tell us about Robert." I had been dying to grill her on the subject all week.

"Let's just say Jess, he knows his way around a woman's body."

I had always had that feeling about him, but that was probably because of what he kept telling me time and time again as he lurked behind me at the photocopier.

"He is very conscious of my needs." She says already starting to slur her words.

I'm already beginning to feel light-headed, but I keep drinking, regardless. I fall backwards into a beanbag and get wedged.

"Help!" I shout across to them and Abbey and Hazel each take a hand and pull me out again. I spice things up by mixing up cocktails. I make Abbey and Hazel a Mojito's each and I settle on my usual Long Island Iced Tea. I put on Maroon 5 and show them my moves like Jagger. Hazel goes down to the floor in a slut drop, only to pull something in her back on the way up. She takes a good five minutes to get back on her feet again. Abbey is incredibly giggly now and just sits in an armchair laughing to herself and enjoying the show. A couple of hours later we are doing the conga around the back garden. None of us really sure how we got there.

"I'm getting married in the morning. Ding-dong, the bells are gonna chime."

"It's not tomorrow, is it? The wedding, I mean." Hazel says not really sure what she is doing let alone what day of the week it is.

"Abbey. Tell me I'm not getting married tomorrow... am I?"

"Don't take my word for anything. Not at the moment." Abbey slurs.

We make our way back to the house somehow. I think we might have crawled on our hands and knees judging by the state of mine.

"What is Joseph like then?" Hazel asks curiously. "You know, in the bedroom department?

"Terrible." I say, trying to look serious. In fact, he's so bad I have to make him do it again and again just to make sure. Much in the same way that you have to keep eating chocolate just to make sure it still tastes as nice. I'm just helping to hone his skills, that's all. That's how I look at it. I'm doing him a big favour.

"He's amazing," I say "I wouldn't be marrying him otherwise. In fact, he's the most wonderful man I've ever met."

I am now crying and very drunk. We all have a group hug and then call it a night. Hazel and Abbey collapse in the spare room while I sleep in my bedroom at the front of the house. An hour later, I hear something at the window. I wake up with a start, not quite sure what is going on. I stagger over to the window and open the blind. Joseph is stood outside at the gate looking up at me. His eyes are lost amidst a midnight blue background. I can see David and his dad sitting on the bench in the park. I open the window, still swaying slightly.

"I love you!" I shout in a very loud voice, but thinking I am talking very quietly.

"We heard that." says John from across the road.

"I think everyone in the street heard that." says David laughing.

"They were supposed to." I say shouting again.

"I love you too," Joseph says. "I will see you tomorrow." he says smiling and blowing me a kiss.

"Are we getting married tomorrow? I can't remember"

"No," he says, "not tomorrow. It's next weekend."

"That is good news," I say, breathing a huge sigh of relief. "only I've had a couple of drinks."

"I would never have guessed!"

"It's just I forgot to eat today, so it's gone to my head. I shall see you in my dreams." I say as I trip and almost disappear from view. "It's alright I didn't fall."

"Try not to injure yourself. We don't want you ending up with a broken leg, do we?"

"Can't you come up and keep me company. I'm all alone in this big bed. I have needs."

"The only thing you need is to sleep it off. Besides, I will be over first thing in the morning to give you everything you need."

I make my best attempt to look sad as I wave and close the

window. Despite my qualms, I fall fast asleep as soon as my head touches the pillow.

The next morning, I wake up with one of Celine's bad heads. I Think she must have lent it to me for the day. Abbey and Hazel both look as awful as me. After they have been picked up by their respective partner's I am left to assess the damage from the night before. The doorbell rings. I look at him on my phone as he is pouting into the camera, almost steaming it up with his hot breath. He is like a sexy delivery driver, and I have to say that his package is rather impressive.

I open the door and practically drag him in. It is not him I am lusting for at this moment, but the rye sourdough he has just picked up from Waitrose for me. He also has a box of painkillers and other breakfast goodies, which he is planning to cook up a storm with. My post breakfast goodies would have to be kept on hold for now. He produces something really quite good, and I do my best to clear my plate. We seem to have the wedding preparations under control. We both have Friday off to iron out any last-minute hitches.

"Let's just laze about today." I say, feeling a bit lacklustre.

"Sounds good to me." he says. We watch a couple of films, or rather he does. I just lie on him and go to sleep. He picks us up a curry to eat in the evening from our favourite Indian

Restaurant across the road. I am feeling a bit better now, so I start to perk up a bit. We go upstairs to read in bed.

"Thanks for today," I say smiling at him, "you're so good to me". He kisses me, then continues playing solitaire. I smile to myself and fall asleep contentedly.

The Biggest Surprise

If I thought last week went quickly, this week absolutely flies by. I can't believe it is already Thursday afternoon.

Alan gathers us together upstairs as everyone congratulates me and I get handed an envelope with John Lewis vouchers inside it.

"Thanks everyone." I say, feeling a bit emotional.

I just have a small sip of wine and then pack up my cards in the boot of the car. When I get home, Joseph is there waiting for me. He did promise he would try to get home early tonight.

"I'm all yours." He says walking towards me.

"You better be!" I say, throwing my arms around him.

"Anton has everything ready. He will lay it all out while we are at the church."

"Not everything I hope!" I say, and we both start to laugh. We have been invited to Celine and John's for dinner. When we get there, Celine has cooked a lovely casserole complete with seasonal vegetables and warm bread rolls.

"Not long now you too." Celine says, smiling all over her

face. "How exciting!"

I on the other hand have got to the point where it will be a relief when it is all over. I am feeling completely exhausted I know Joseph is too.

"It's so nice of you to do this for us, Mum." Joseph says putting his arms around her.

"My pleasure" she says grinning at us both. "Don't worry about a thing Jess," she says, "we have all been assigned our duties with strict instructions to leave you to relax as much as possible."

"I might take you up on that." I say, already yawning and stretching.

We finish dinner and Joseph and I head back to the house for an early night. I climb into bed and quickly go off to sleep. Leaving Joseph making yet more lists to cross off.

I must have slept in as I wake up to an empty house. I go downstairs and switch on the Christmas lights before making my first cup of tea. I sit and eat a leisurely breakfast before disappearing for a shower. I get dressed and just doze on the sofa in the conservatory, looking out of the window at the garden. I will be spending the night in my own house with my family, which will be just like old times. I am looking forward to getting ready there tomorrow before the wedding. Everyone is due to arrive later today and will be sleeping in my spare bedrooms. My lonely house will be full once more.

As I make another cup of tea in the kitchen, I spot activity outside. I think this warrant's further investigation of the Miss Marple variety. I throw on my chunky jumper, clip my hair up on top of my head and rush out of the back door. The dogs are going bonkers running around barking and wagging their tails furiously. I spy Joseph standing with his arms folded across his chest. He is talking to the guys that are putting up the marquis.

"Watch out here comes trouble," I hear one of them say.

"I wondered when you would make an appearance." Joseph says with sarcasm in his voice.

"How about when you decide to let me know where you are. You left your phone at home."

"Oh, sorry." he says all apologetic, "The weather forecast isn't great, so they got here early just in case."

He puts his arms around me and kisses me lingeringly on the lips. "Do you think it's too late to change my mind?" he says teasingly.

"If you want to retain both of your testicles, then yes.

Besides, it was too late the moment you laid eyes on me. I'm far too irresistible." I say tossing my head back.

"Far too modest as well by the look of things." He says smiling.

"Young love," Celine says. "Do you remember when we were like that, John?"

"Yes, dear." John says nodding and smiling at his wife in agreement. I think she could ask John anything and he would give the same answer. She smiles and goes back to what she was doing. I can't believe this is really happening. I am giddy and completely overcome with excitement. I do a scissor kick in the air. Mainly because I know Joseph is watching me walk into the house.

"I'd hate to see her when she's happy." one man says to Joseph cheekily. But he is lost in thoughts of his own and just smiles in their direction.

I enter the house to see Celine moving like a tornado rushing from one room to the next. I felt dizzy just from watching her.

"Anything I can do to help?" I ask her as she dashes past. Just wander around and check everything looks okay. She says in a nervous voice.

"It all looks amazing," I say, scanning the room for specks of dust, "you must have been at it for hours?"

"I got John up at 4:30 because I was having trouble sleeping." Lucky John, he must be so grateful I know I would be. "I was just lying-in bed worrying myself to death about everything."

"Oh, Celine!" I say and put my arms around her. "Thank you for everything you and John are doing. How about I make us a nice cup of tea and we crack open the mince pies?"

"Thank you. That would be lovely. I am feeling tired, come to think of it."

"We will sit back and admire your handy work from a couple of comfy chairs." I say walking to the kitchen.

One cup turns into eight as everyone outside decides they want one as well. I find a large tray with flowers on it and fill it will eight mugs and a large stack of mince pies. I then make my way back to Celine where I pass her, her tea and mince pie before heading outside. Joseph hands them out so I can go back inside in the warmth as I'm feeling the chill through my jumper. We sit back and admire Celine's work for a moment. The house looks beautiful. It is filled to the brim with foliage and flowers in shades of lilac, pink and white. There is ivy cascading down the side of the planters. We will serve the wedding breakfast in the marquis but will hopefully move into the house in the evening. It is already beginning to take shape as people turn their attention to the inside. They are laying out various tables for the cake and buffet. Yet again, impressive planters fill the area with scent and beauty.

"Are you happy with everything, darling?" Celine questions me.

"What do you think?" I say in reply. We are both shedding a few tears as Joseph decides to poke his head around the door.

"Is this a private party or can anyone join in?" He says sniffing a bit himself. He too is a bit overcome with the enormity of it all.

"I have just taken leave of your Christmas present." I say this to tease him because I know he hasn't had time to shop for me yet and I want to see the look of sheer panic on his face.

He then says, "What have you been doing? I got your present weeks ago!" It is his turn to laugh as the colour drains from my cheeks. Well, that backfired on me, I think to myself.

"He's kidding can't you tell by now? He told us you two haven't had time to shop for presents for one another." says Celine trying to put my mind at rest.

"I've just bought you something small to open when we get back from our honeymoon."

Something small for him could be a new TT. He'd say, 'but its only small', 'small in stature but not in value'.

"I think I'm going to pop out," I say bidding them goodbye, "I have last minute shopping to do in town."

I set across the park to my house. I set the car to defrost while I drink a hot mug of tea on the doorstep. It isn't as much fun driving a sports car in this weather. Even I'm not brave enough to put the top down on a day like today. I shall have to listen to my music by myself rather than blasting it in everyone else's lugholes. I throw on a scarf and hat and jump into the now warm, unfrozen car. I feel sad as I think of my lovely house now lying dormant. It has been dwarfed by a different home. Never mind, it would later be filled to the rafters with my visiting relatives. For which I have everything primed and ready to go.

I have filled the fridge up with tasty things for breakfast and treats for later. Each bed has a pile of clean towels at the end of it. I have even placed a mint on each pillow as a little joke. I head off in the direction of town, along with everyone else who lives within a three-mile radius of it. I am annoyed for not buying him his present's sooner. I park on the outskirts and go the rest of the way on foot. I walk along the treelined road and over the familiar level crossing which runs through the town. Congratulating myself for getting through without the signals lighting up and flashing red, indicating a train is on its way. The walk has really focused my mind and I am currently a woman on a mission.

I rush into Ernest Jones (other jewellers are available, just not in this town). I buy him a set of Mont Blanc cuff links. Maybe he can wear these tomorrow if we decide to open presents early. I head for the local department store where I buy him a Chanel gift set complete with mini atomiser for the gym and a Ralph Lauren sweater. I can't find a balaclava for his wall scaling escapade so a beanie hat courtesy of Ralph L will have to do. I will be able to see exactly who it is but, after all, I wouldn't want any nasty surprises. Any more cases of mistaken identity. The previous one would last me a lifetime. I want to know exactly who is infiltrating my drawbridge before they do it.

I head to the fitness store where I purchase copious amounts of protein bars of every colour and flavour to be arranged in a wicker hamper later on. They should keep him going for a while. Half an hour later, I am finished. That ladies and gentlemen is how it's done. Right, onwards and upwards.

I walk back to the car with a spring in my step. I am satisfied that Christmas shopping is now well and truly crossed off the list. There doesn't seem to be a cloud in the sky, so I'm not sure what Joseph meant when he spoke about the weather forecast. I complete the McDonald's drive through picking up a few of his favourites. I'm sure he won't have had time to fix himself lunch. I begin to feel nervous. I had just consumed two chocolate twists courtesy of Costa and I am now suffering from consumer's remorse. What if I couldn't fit into my wedding dress? Jessica Rabbit would have a spare tyre or two to try to conceal. Not quite the look I was going for. I race back to the house before Joseph's food goes cold. He smiles when he sees the brown paper bag I am carrying.

"You must have read my mind," he says, smiling.

"It is coming quite naturally to me now." I tell him.

"What am I thinking now?" He says flashing me that sexy smile of his.

I hand him the bag with the black hat and a box of Milk Tray and say, "See if you can work out what I have in mind? I just hope you have sufficient grips on your trainers."

I hum the song from the advert. He begins to piece everything together, judging by the look of sheer terror on his face.

"Can you see if you can borrow a ladder from someone it might make things easier? I'll make it worth your while." I say as I wiggle my bottom and wave him goodbye.

"Can I eat my lunch first?" he asks, biting into his burger.

"Desserts on me, or you." I haven't decided yet.

Possibly both of us. All would be revealed in due course. I would allow all my comments to percolate whilst I went off to stash his Christmas presents before he got back to the house with mine. I just hope he puts the bow around it. I turn on the tv only to find out that Sister Act, another of my personal favourites, is in full swing. I make myself another mug of tea and plonk myself down on the sofa. Life doesn't get any better than this. Tomorrow I am marrying the man of my dreams and now Woopy Goldberg to boot. I am just joining the nuns for a good old sing song when I hear a strange noise. A sort of knocking coming from outside somewhere.

I look out and see a ladder being placed against the rear wall of the house. I can feel the all too familiar tingle again. I just hope it's not the window cleaner that would be really disappointing. Sure enough, now clad in a black sweater and beanie hat, Joseph is scaling the ladder destined for the bedroom. His dad is stood at the bottom holding it steady. It is not quite the romantic frisson I had in mind, but it would have to do. I just hope John doesn't decide to follow him up. It could get rather awkward. I dash upstairs and fly to the bedroom window to open it. He shouts up that he is here to give me my Christmas present. "Did you put a bow around it?" I ask, smiling.

"Damn. I knew there was something I had to do. When I wasn't scaling a ladder risking live and limb."

The ladder starts to wobble and slide to the left, at which time my heart is in my mouth. I haven't had this much excitement in ages. He manages to grab hold of a bit of nearby drainpipe while he steadies the ladder. I kiss him as he practically falls in through the window onto the floor below. I call down to John.

"I will take it from here thanks."

"Right you are." he says, making a hasty retreat back towards the house. We literally roll about on the floor laughing.

"I'm sure there are better uses of my time," he says, trying to look serious. "one day I'm CEO of a successful company, the next day I am 'Milk Tray Man' climbing up a rear wall to get into my own house."

"When you put it like that," I say trying to console him, "at least I keep you grounded," I say defensively. "Or not. As the case might be. Anyway, wouldn't you rather be doing this than working?"

I smile and undress him. I kiss him while he undresses me. Just then I ask, "Wait a minute, where are the chocolates?"

"Is that all you care about?"

"Hold that thought," I dash downstairs and come back clutching a pot of chocolate sauce, "this will just have to do. Once I have covered you in this, I will have to do a very thorough job to get it all off. I must warn you; we could be here for hours!"

I cover my finger in chocolate sauce and gently spread it around his mouth. I then slowly remove it with my tongue. I then make him laugh by drawing two camo stripes on my face. One either side of my nose. As I head down his body, I picture myself walking down the aisle in my now even tighter dress. Maybe I won't cover him in the whole lot this time. As I place a small amount around the end of him, he places his hands behind his head and closes his eyes. My chocolate fantasy is complete.

After we have removed the last of the chocolate sauce, we take a shower and head back to check on things at Celine and

John's by now all the hard work is done. The marquis is complete and dressed to perfection. I am just waiting for my family to arrive to make everything picture perfect. My phone rings and it is my parents calling me from the airport just to let me know that they have arrived safely and should be with me in an hour or so. My two brothers have texted to say they are both on their way. Everything was starting to come together at last. An hour later, my parents arrive. They are so tanned I hardly recognise them. They are completely bowled over when they meet Joseph.

"Who's a pretty boy then?" My mum says looking him up and down.

"You sound surprised!" I say in an irritated voice. Although she has made him sound as if he should be in a cage sharpening his beak on a cuttlefish.

"There was that one," she begins to say. But I quickly cut her off.

"I know the one you mean. I don't want to talk about it. I needed an eye test. Let's leave it at that shall we?"

Luckily Joseph and my dad are chatting happily about cars. I really don't want to talk about my old boyfriend in front of him the day before we are tying the knot. Just in the nick of time, my two brothers arrive in a screeching of brakes. They are like buses. Nothing and then two at once. One of my brothers is with his partner, the other one is by himself.

"Teresa has fallen down the stairs and is covered head to toe in bruises. So, she is resting at home and she sends her love."

"Some people will do anything to get out of a wedding!" I say laughing.

Before Joseph can open his mouth, I shout "Don't get any idea's!"

"Would I?" he says, looking the picture of innocence. "Jess did that," says Joseph, "Went face down on a leaf blower she had inadvertently placed at the bottom of the stairs!"

"Let's leave it there, shall we?" I say, shooting him a look. Joseph's answer was to bring me a medical kit from the cupboard posing as the hunky paramedic. He then told me I might feel a little prick or in this case a very large one. He could have just helped me up, but his antics helped to take my mind off my injuries for a while.

By now my family has taken him well and truly under their wing. Including him in all the banter and private jokes. He has an incredible knack of being able to get on with anyone of any class or standing. He just switches it up or down as required. My family has a great sense of humour. Luckily, I have already broken him in along with his mum and dad otherwise he wouldn't have of had a clue what we were talking about as there are a lot of in jokes. I keep going over every last detail for tomorrow in my mind. Trying to make sure nothing has been missed.

Celine has taken hold of the rings. She is under my strict instructions not to hand them over to David until the last minute. If he looks as if he is up to something, she is quite happy to take him down. This time without the colourful language but only if he tries something in the church if it's at her house then it is no holds barred. I am keeping our first dance a secret from Joseph. If it was up to him, we would dance to 'Fix You' by Coldplay. I have something far more beautiful in mind.

At six o'clock we get up and leave them to it. We are going to the pub later for a family meal before the big day. We are planning to pick John and Celine up on the way. Joseph and I take our familiar route back to the house. It is hard to believe it has only been a few months since we first met. It seems more like a lifetime ago. This bench will remain in my memory always as we have sat together on it so many times. We have one last kiss against the tree for old times' sake.

"We could carve a heart and our initials," I say to him

"And risk the neighbourhood watch giving us an earful. No thanks. We know it's there even if we can't see it."

"Yes, it is." I say looking at him lovingly.

"I love you," says Joseph, "all of you that is."

"Even my big bottom?" I say pushing it out for him to slap.

"Your family, I mean."

"Oh well, they love you. It was never in doubt as far as I'm concerned."

We go inside and spruce ourselves up. I wash my hair and let the curls dry naturally. I throw on a tight knitted dress and long boots. I put on makeup and give myself a spray of Chanel before making my way downstairs. He stops what he is doing to look at me. I then see him look towards the clock.

"We don't have time for that," I say.

"But you look so gorgeous," he says. "can't I just …?"

"No," I say pushing his hand away, "You'll have to wait until tomorrow."

He huffs and says, "Alright. I'll wait until tomorrow."

"It will make it all the sweeter." I say attempting to pacify him.

"Me covered in chocolate sauce; it doesn't get any sweeter than that."

"Think that's sweet. Watch and learn baby," I say spurred on by his bigheadedness.

I walk over to him. Hoist up my dress and sits on his lap with one leg either side of him. I then place his hands on my breasts while I smother his mouth with hungry, open-mouthed kisses. I get up laughing as he visibly struggles to catch his breath.

"You have a real pinkness to your cheeks," I hear him say.

"I'm probably still bruised from where you slammed me down on the bathroom counter," I say laughing.

 "Not those cheeks. Your face!"

"I'm trying out a new face cream it is supposed to give you a healthy glow." I explain to him.

What I omit to tell him is that I'm pregnant and that we are in fact embarking on a shotgun wedding. Technically speaking that is. I will just let him think that Joe junior wants to be with his daddy so much that he arrives early. Carrying his child seemed to be making everything more intense. More intense than a chocolate fondant with an oozing molten centre. I'm guessing that we must have hit the bullseye first time, that's all I can say.

There is a lot of noise and commotion outside signalling the arrival of said family members. We lock up and head out to greet them. I will lay off the alcohol from now on the pretence that I wish to keep a clear head for tomorrow. I am a vessel for the most precious cargo I have ever carried. I seem to get away with it this time. No-one seems to suspect a thing. I imagine that Celine has noticed something, but I think I must be imaging things. I don't want her rushing out to buy baby clothes just yet. Lucky for me the wedding isn't in a month or two. I think I am going to get enormous judging by the serious chocolate cravings that I am already suffering from. Mind you, who am I kidding? I've been having those all my life, why should now be any different. My sister-in-law Cindy tells me how well I look. I feel myself going paler as she says it.

"I put that down to Mr perfect and his equally perfect you know what," I say lying through my teeth.

"He hasn't got a twin brother, has he?" she asks hopefully.

"Celine and John broke the mould when they made him."

"Shame" she says, looking thoughtful. He looks over at us and smiles.

"We're talking about you, not to you," she says teasing him.

"In that case I'll leave you to it," he says politely and carries on talking about cars and brake horsepower.

I am all too aware that I will not be spending the night with him. I will miss him terribly. At the same time, he has had a few drinks. The snoring is something I will not miss one bit. I may even be able to hear it from my house across the road.

Everyone is incredibly jolly as we leave the pub. My mum and Celine are chatting happily while walking along arm in arm. Joseph decides to recreate the kiss we shared on our night out with David and Abbey. Yet again we are left in a state of breathlessness. I think mine is partly down to the amount of beer fumes that are being omitted as he opens his mouth.

"I'm merely getting into the spirit of things." He says defending himself, "It is nearly Christmas after all."

"Not for another twenty-five hours, but we won't argue about it." We look up at a nearby lamppost and spot flakes of snow starting to come down.

"It's snowing!" everyone behind us shouts at the same time.

I will just have to wear wellies under my dress instead, I sigh to myself. The girls will be happy, they will get to wear their pink fluffy boots. I wouldn't have put it past them to have asked their magic unicorns to make this happen. Oh well, at least they will be happy. Making snow angels in their bridesmaid dresses before we go inside the church. Joseph starts a rendition of I'm dreaming of a white Christmas closely followed by the rest of us. I say goodbye to Joseph.

"Until we meet again," he says, kissing my hand and bowing. "Now for the hard bit."

I smile, knowing that the hard bit has already been done. He just doesn't know it yet.

The Big Day

When I wake up, I am feeling a little shell-shocked. I head downstairs in a daze to find everyone frantically rushing about. My sister-in-law, Cindy, is trying to locate hair straighteners. Someone else has their head in the fridge searching for a packet of bacon. I head into the garden to walk about for a bit. My last-minute nerves are starting to get the better of me again. It's 9:30, and the wedding is at 12:30. I still have three hours to kill. What I don't realise, having never got married before, is that time flies by without you noticing. What seems like only five minutes later, everyone is assembled downstairs waiting for me to appear.

After arguing with myself, I decide to wear my hair up and allow a couple of curls to tumble down at the sides. I place pretty shiny hair clips here and there. I put on some light makeup and douse myself in Chanel. Last but not least, I put on the necklace Celine has leant me. It is a beautiful diamond and topaz pendant. Which is a coincidence as my favourite colour is turquoise! My dress fits like a dream despite all my fears. Not a paunch in sight or a baby bump, come to that. The sumptuous silk skims and hugs my curvy figure. I take one last deep breath and with my heart beating out of my chest force open the living room door. My mum and Cindy both take a sharp intake of breath.

"Wow!" my dad says, "He is a lucky boy!"

My hands shake as I shift nervously around the room. I decide to rest on the piano stool. I run my fingers across the keys where his have been countless times. It is the closest I can get to holding his hand right now. Which is of course what I really need to do? So much so that it aches deep inside me. It is 12:15 as I spot a dark blue car pulling up outside. I can see the girls jumping around excitedly in the back. I can imagine David plying them with E-numbers before placing them in the car and sending them over. Another one of his little jokes.

This was it. The moment of truth has arrived. I put on the cloak and gloves and now all I needed was the driver to play the theme from rocky and I would be set. I give myself a pep talk. This is going to be the fight of my life and I am ready. In fact, I was born ready. As we slowly make our way to the church, the others follow in the car behind. The driver takes the long route to make sure we do not arrive at the church before the groom.

The snow had stopped an hour or so after it started, so all that is left is a light dusting of icing sugar on the pavements outside. As I walk down the Aisle arm in arm with my dad. I feel as though someone else has taken leave of my body. Just as I look up, he turns his head towards me. The organ is playing out, I try to keep it together, but his eyes look as though they are twinkling just for me in an even deeper shade of blue than ever before. With this beautiful backdrop I imagine them to be a heavenly shade of blue. He looks incredible in his top hat. I reprimand myself for trying to turn a beautiful moment into something else.

He turns to me and whispers "Stunning Stanning", I realise this is the last time anyone will call me that. It will be Mrs Matthews from now on and I couldn't be happier about it. The church looks exquisite and the stained glass is looking freshly polished as the sun shines through it. I wonder if Celine has been up there with a duster. Breathing on them, bringing them to a lovely shine. Suddenly we reach the important bit.

"First, I am required to ask anyone present who knows a reason why these persons may not lawfully marry, to declare it now?" asks the vicar.

I look at David and then back at Abbey who is mouthing out to me "He wouldn't dare," and he doesn't.

As we exchange rings, a tear escapes and trickles down my cheek. He just wipes it away with his hand as the vicar tells him he can now kiss the bride. We just rub noses before planting a delicate kiss on one another's lips. Hand in hand, we walk off to do the paperwork. David and Abbey stand to one side as I sit down to sign first. I suddenly have a memory blank and can't remember what my own name is. Do I sign the old one or the new one? I had already tried to put his ring on the wrong finger. Finally, it comes back to me. Joseph sits down and scans the document, perhaps checking for the get-out clause.

David shouts, "Just sign it already. It's not a business contract."

When the vicar says "This is the most important contract of all. The one with god."

Joseph quickly signs the paperwork and heads out of the vestry. We walk out of the church to be met by a sea of confetti, most of which swirls around before deciding to take up residence in my hair. We look like a couple of monkeys as Joseph spends the next five minutes picking each bit out of it. We pose next to trees and foliage as the photographer clicks away with his camera. It is not long before Joseph drives us back to the house accompanied by Nigel, who of course is looking amazing with a crisp white satin bow on his blue bonnet.

"You look incredible," he says.

"So, do you!" I say back, "Your eyes have never looked better."

"That, my dear wife, is because they like what they see. Very much!"

Anton had done us proud. The food looks really wonderful. We had decided against a roast in favour of a buffet. What with it being Christmas the next day. Besides, we would be on a beach somewhere sunning ourselves, anyway. Everyone helped themselves to food while they chatted easily with one-another and the champagne flowed. I kept pretending to drink mine. I didn't have to worry as my mum was busy drinking up all the half-empty glasses which is her party piece and one which I was incredibly grateful for as it was digging me out of hole. It was time for the speeches.

David keeps his very short and sweet. He explains how he thought Joseph and I might be a mistake, but it had turned out to be the best mistake Joseph had ever made. I feel relieved as it comes to an end. My dad generally waffles on and tries to embarrass me by talking about my previous boyfriend's saying that Joseph was the best out of the bunch. There is a compliment in there somewhere, I am sure. Joseph thanks me for making him the happiest man in the entire world.

I stand up and say I have just three words to say, "He

completes me." before quickly sitting back down again.

The time has come for our much anticipated first dance. Joseph waits to see what it is and is greeted by the silken tones of Sam Smith and Lay Me Down. One of the most beautiful songs ever written in my opinion. I am filled with happy memories of the two of us snuggled up in bed, not the sad ones of that retched fateful day.

"I thought you might have chosen Another Love by Tom Odell?"

"Too sad," I say.

"I Can't Make You Love Me?"

"Too depressing," I tell him, "This one is just right."

"Okay, Goldilocks." he says clutching me in a warm embrace. "I'll tell you what is not too big, not too small and just right."

I shake my head and look away. Our second wedding song is a much more joyous affair. I have selected Never Knew Love Like This Before by Jody.

We shoulder shimmy back and forth in time to the music as everyone else jumps up and joins in.

"Are you going to tell me where we are going on

honeymoon?" I ask him excitedly.

"Ah, about that," I sense a but coming.

"You didn't book anything."

"I did, but it might not be what you were expecting, that's all. A bit colder, maybe. How about Paris? I thought we could have a hot sultry number later in the year."

"When I'm heavily pregnant, you mean?"

"Sorry, I wasn't really thinking. Besides, we will have a good time wherever we go, you know that."

"Okay, I forgive you." I say, kissing him on the mouth and stroking his face.

"Phew," he says, "I've been so worried."

"Well, worry no more. I love the idea". What I was really feeling was drained. As I escape to the loo, I meet Abbey in the hallway.

"You okay, Jess. You don't look so good. Are you unwell or something,"?

"Not unwell," I say "pregnant."

"Oh wow, that's splendid news, isn't it?"

"Yes, but you can't tell anyone. Not even David. I just

really needed someone to talk to."

"You can always talk to me. You know that. Does Joseph know?"

"Know what?" He says from behind me.

"I was just telling Jess our good news." Abbey says, "We've decided to get the girls a puppy."

"Oh wow. David never said. I'll leave you to it then," he says, disappearing.

"Are you feeling sick?" she asks me

"Not yet, should I be?"

"You might be one of the lucky ones. I felt bad both times with mine. Sore boobs anything like that?"

"Not yet, but it is early days."

"Yes," she says, "you've got so much to look forward to."

"Sounds like it." I say, forcing a smile.

It is now time for us to leave. I have to quickly repack my suitcase, exchanging summer clothes for winter woollies. We say goodbye to John and Celine.

John says, "Have a good time you too. Don't do anything I wouldn't do!"

Celine says to me, "Be gentle with him. You don't have to be too gentle, if you get my meaning, but I want him back in one piece. Him and that adorable face of his. Capiche," she says, going all Sopranos on me.

"Understood" I tell her. We jump in the taxi and make our way to the airport. "Damn!" I shout out.

"What?" he says, looking worried.

"I forgot to give them their Christmas presents."

"Oh, don't worry about that. They have a key. I will phone them later and tell them where to find them." I panic. I think the pregnancy test is at the bottom of the bin. I'm sure I buried it so it will be okay. The flight takes off and we are there before we know it.

"This was a good idea of yours," I say lovingly to him.

"It means we will get straight down to business. Of the baby making variety."

"Is that all I am to you, a baby machine?" I ask him.

"No, but it's a start." Joseph says smiling his special smile. Yet again I have started without you, I think to myself.

Paris in December

When we arrive at the hotel room the first thing, I do, is run a bath. I climb into the warm water and close my eyes as I drift off.

"Hey sleepy head." He is wearing a shirt, top hat, and nothing else.

"I thought you had to hand that back?"

"Not this one. I bought this one ages ago for a trip to the races."

I perk myself up a bit. It would be rude not to considering all the effort he has gone to. I make myself look ravishing and follow him to the bedroom. He is lying on his side with his hand under his chin, pretending to drink from a cup and saucer. I Feel as though someone has attached a defibrillator to my lower regions and has just shouted "clear" and I am now feeling the aftereffects as a stream of sexual electricity rips through me.

"Wow"! I say as I walk in. "You don't disappoint." He just manages to place down the teacup and saucer as I launch myself at him.

"Shall I take the hat off?" he asks gently.

"No, leave it exactly where it is," I say snogging his face off. He places it on my head. "where have you gone?" I say, holding out my hands to find him. I'm not saying he has a big head, but his hat sits halfway down my face.

"Sorry." he says laughing and launching the hat across the room like a frisbee.

"Where was I?" He asks. Burying his face in my neck.

I lie back and let him make all my problems disappear. It must be the top hat image. All we need is a magic wand, and I know exactly where I can lay my hands on one of those. We lie back on the bed and the only thing missing is a cigar which he has swapped for an iPad, which is gratification in technical form. He puts his arm around me, and I cuddle into him.

"Which one of your depraved fantasies will we be carrying out next? How about Spiderman?" he suggests

"I hate spiders."

"I could run around the house getting rid of all the spiders for you."

"You do that anyway and don't think I haven't noticed how frightened you are."

"I could go for Superman."

"You could fly me upstairs, throw me on the bed and let me bounce off."

"You're not going to let me forget that are you?"

"Not a chance." I say shaking my head, "How about you? Is there anything you would like me to dress up as?"

"No, not really. You are everything I need. You fulfil all of my fantasies just being you."

"Aw" I say peacefully drifting off to sleep.

Over the next few days, we manage to successfully tick off everything on my list. We take a visit to the Louvre to gaze upon Mona Lisa and I drool over the various Monet paintings on display in the Monet museum. I love his Bridge Over a Pond of Waterlilies painting, which reminds me of a trip Andrew, and I took to visit Monet's house and garden in Giverny. That is where you will find the beautiful bridge over the lily pond. A magical time I just wish Joseph had been there with me.

We have copious amounts of sex while seductively feeding each-other croissants and pain au chocolate, to keep up our strength.

We buy macaroons and various other sweet treats from a patisserie from around the corner; but as there appears to be one of those around every corner, it is hardly surprising!

We light candles from within the beautiful Notre Dame Cathedral and wonder at pavement artists while they paint pictures and caricatures along the Seine. We climb the 647 steps to the top of the Eiffel tower and look out over the City. We walk along a side street and spot a pretty little bistro with a striped awning outside. We sit inside and dine on fillet mignon and pommes-frites followed by crepes, which we feed each-other tenderly. We consider taking a romantic boat trip along the river but decide that a romantic moonlit stroll will do the job just as well.

Besides, we can stop and make each other breathless as often as we like without fear of upsetting anyone. Which we do every five minutes whilst gazing up at the night sky. As we do, I alternate between his eyes and the night sky unable to decide which one is more twinkly than the other. I still think he has the edge just. I have decided to confess about the baby as I am struggling to keep it to myself any longer. It is our last evening in Paris, so we are taking a trip to go ice skating at the Trocadero which looks out across the Seine.

I used to love ice skating when I was a teenager, although I spent more time looking at boys than where I was going. I doubt tonight will be any different except tonight my boy will be stood beside me holding my hand. I lace up my boots and head onto the ice and it all comes back to me quickly and I am soon gliding effortlessly around the ice. It is at this point I suddenly remember I am pregnant. I will just have to be careful and avoid any pile ups that could take me down. Joseph has already decided it is not for him and is laughing at a 'You Tube' video David has sent to him. I carry on gliding and wave up at him, every so often, as I pass by. Afterwards we wonder around a Christmas market which has the smell of all sorts of yummy things like biscuits and pretzels. I take his hand and suggest that we sit down.

"I have something to tell you," I say, looking deadly serious for a change, "I'm pregnant. I've just been waiting for the right moment to tell you."

"How? We have only been here for a few days." He says looking stunned.

I found out just before the wedding. Do you remember that one night of illicit passion where birth control had gone out of the window?

"I must have been on fire that evening," he says in a boasting voice.

"I think it was practically on fire from what I can remember. Judging by the way I was walking the next day."

He laughs out loud at the memory. "You looked as though you'd been riding a donkey."

"Don't be so hard on yourself. I know you can be an ass sometimes, but I like to think of you as more as a stallion." He must be every bit as potent as I thought he might be. I'm surprised I didn't get pregnant the first time he looked at me. "You can't tell anyone as we need to wait another couple of months."

"Okay, it will be our little secret." He says smiling at me.

"Well, Abbeys too technically. I'm sorry I told her at the wedding. I couldn't keep it in any longer."

"So that was what you two were up to. Puppy my arse. David's allergic to dogs, anyway."

Why does that not surprise me? Anyone who doesn't like dogs must be dodgy. Even if it is because they bring him out in a nasty rash. A decent man would just grin and bear it. Besides, that is exactly what he does to me.

"You feel, okay, don't you?" he asks looking concerned. "I didn't think I could be any happier. You've just shattered that theory. I am going to wrap you up in cotton wool and keep you safe from harm."

"Like a mummy I say laughing. Joe juniors mummy

anyway."

"Very good." which is what he had taken to saying at my every attempt at humour. I think he's just jealous that he hasn't thought of it first.

We spend our remaining time in Paris calling each-other Mummy and Daddy, free in the knowledge that no one will overhear or even care for that matter or understand so great is the language barrier. Mind you, I do have problems with accents; I think that everyone is from the same part of the world. I love Gerard Butler, but I would need subtitles as even broad Scottish is beyond me, except Lorraine Kelly but she is a legend so needs no translation. Our honeymoon eventually comes to an end and we board the plane full of hope and sugar. It now ran through our veins due to the large amount we had consumed in such a short space of time.

We still have our gifts to exchange with one another when we get back. His are all wrapped up and waiting in the bedroom. It wouldn't be a first. They are not delicately wrapped in lace this time, but in pretty baskets and ribbons. We prize open the front door and just sit down and collapse. It is surprisingly good to be back home again. I wander around the house and marvel at everything as if it is the first time, I have laid eyes on it. Everything seems to look different somehow. The boys have spied us and are scratching at the back door to come in. Their tails are wagging back and forth like little chocolate-coloured pendulums. I picture the countdown clock in my mind and the music signalling that time is up and wonder if their tails could keep in time with the music.

Joseph unlocks the door and carefully unleashes them, ensuring that they don't knock me over in their excitement. Soon we will have our own little boy to look after, or so we hoped. Joseph will exchange sad looking tennis balls for ones of the football variety. He has already started thinking that when the baby starts to kick, he might be able to hold a football up to my stomach and the baby will somehow miraculously kick it back to him. Just wishful thinking on his part so great is his impatience to be with his son. He is suitably impressed with all the gifts I have given him and immediately opens a protein bar and starts to demolish it while I just stand and watch him mesmerised.

"I think I've earned this."

I just nod and cross my legs. He returns carrying a small gift box, which I open to reveal the most beautiful diamond earrings I have ever seen.

"They are wonderful," I say to him. "The only problem is

I don't have pierced ears."

"Sorry,", he says, shrugging. "I thought all women had them?"

"A lot do, but we aren't born with them. I shall get them pierced just for you. Anyway, it's the thought that counts." I say, stroking his hand. We go up to have an early night as we both need to get up early in the morning.

A Different Corner

Hazel thinks there is something different about me that she can't put her finger on. She decides to put it all down to married bliss. So, I sit back and say nothing to alter her opinion. Abbey is checking in on me constantly. She assures me she is counting the weeks. "Are you feeling sick yet?"

"No." I say

"He must be bloody perfect, just like his father. Or so close it frightens him." thinking about his father's pen holder in his study. We laugh and decide Joe's perfectness is to be a foregone conclusion. How could he be anything else?

"That's my son you're talking about. I don't mind your slagging off the husband but leave the kid out of it." We start to laugh again. Joseph has taken to talking to my stomach more than he talks to me.

"I am here!" I say to him in an irritated voice.

"I can talk to you anytime, but it will be Joe's bedtime soon." I decide to let it go for the sake of my unborn child.

I make a doctor's appointment to get it all made official. The midwife is a very serious-looking lady of a bigger build. She just sits and eyes me up and down, trying to decide if I am parent material or not. I decide to confess to her that I may have inadvertently had a few drinks before the wedding. Explaining we only did it the once I didn't realise it could happen so quickly. How do you think pregnancies occur she says making me feel like a complete imbecile? I guess she does have a point; I think to myself. She then goes on to question me by asking how big my husband is. I am just deciding whether to give the answer in inches or centimetres when she says again.

"How tall is he?" she says in an irritated voice

"He is 6ft 2 and well built." I say, smiling.

She then goes on to say, "Why do you petite women choose to be impregnated by these tall, strapping men. Don't you realise the baby has to come out?"

She is yet to meet my husband, but when she does, she will know exactly why I let him impregnate me. It wasn't the size of his baby I was thinking about at the time. Well, not the one he was making with me. I tell Joseph about it later and he says,

"Just take no notice. She probably hasn't had any fun in the last twenty years."

I wonder when someone last put their dibber in her hole.

I laugh and put it to the back of mind. I have, what can only be described as, a pregnancy bible. I fall asleep with it clutched to my chest most nights. I feel as though I am cramming for an exam and already failing somehow. There was so much to learn. I am now nearly eight weeks, so I decide to do my ironing to celebrate. Strange, I know, but I have taken to attempting to be the perfect wife and mother. Constantly ironing shirts and tidying drawers. I iron Josephs shirts for the week, then reach to put the ironing board away.

As I do so, I get a sharp pain in my back. That's strange, I think to myself, and here comes another one. I usually only get those at the beginning of my period and I'm not having those at the moment or anytime soon come to that. I head to the loo having chain drunk three mugs of tea. I always like to have a least one mug on the go, sometimes more.

I notice blood and immediately think to myself this can't be good. I decide not to call Joseph and call the doctor instead to make an appointment for the next day, by the time Joseph returns from work I am now in the throes of a heavy painful period. The pain now having spread to my stomach and pelvis. I don't quite know how to break it to him. So, I say in a tiny voice, "I'm so sorry" My bottom lip quivering like Julia Roberts when she tells Richard Gere about his numerous special gifts.

"What is it?" But I can see he has guessed straight away and runs over to me. He rubs my back and strokes my hair, I don't look at him, but I can tell he is crying.

I head along for my doctor's appointment the next day. Joseph insists on driving me but waits outside in the car at my request. By the end of it the male doctor seems to be almost as upset as me and we console each-other as I close the door behind me. It turns out I have to go into hospital for tests and possibly a small operation.

I am going to have my chimney swept as the doctor politely put it. What he means to say is they are going to remove what is left of my son. They can do what they like to me, providing they knock me out first as I am in so much discomfort now. We go to the hospital for an ultra-sound and they confirm that I am no longer pregnant but that there is a thickening of the womb which they need to rectify. Which means it probably was my fault after all. Trust me to be the one to let the side down. They estimate me to be about twelve weeks that's four more than I thought. It does seem to make sense, as twelve weeks is the dodgy time in pregnancy terms. If you can progress further than that things become a little more certain. I will need to return the next day for the procedure.

I arrive at the hospital wearing the dungarees that I had

taken to wearing. Not because I had to, as there had been no baby bump to speak of, I just enjoyed feeling pregnant, having looked forward to it for so long. I have the procedure and due to a mix-up, they take me to the maternity ward along with the other mothers and their new-born babies. I just lie on the bed listening to two other mothers talking about me.

One of them is asking the other one, "Where is her baby?"

The other replies "I think she lost it."

Making it sound as though it is something I have carelessly misplaced. They are feeling sorry for me and it is more than I can bare. At this point I lose it, just as my baby had turned up to collect me.

"Let's get out of here" he says, his nostrils going into overdrive as his anger is laid bare for all to see.

We treat ourselves to a McDonald's on the way home. We decide to eat in for a change to avoid being alone with one another in the empty house. Neither of us knows how to put what we are feeling into words.

He decides to break the ice by asking, "Are you feeling better now?"

"A bit" I say giving him a faint hint of a smile. I reprimand myself. How can I feel better when I have just lost him, his baby? I don't have a right to feel better. As soon as we get home, I go straight to bed. I just lie there and cry until in a state of exhaustion I fall asleep.

I lie to my boss when he calls and tell him I have a stomach bug. Covers a multitude, that one. He is very kind and gives me the rest of the week off. Alan his boss knows the truth and smooths things over. Joseph carries on working, still unable to face me at the moment and in doing so is allowing me to carry the burden all by myself. Which is the last thing I need? I spend my days gazing at the TV wrapped up in a blanket. Alternating between blowing my nose and drinking vast amounts of tea. I have two unexpected guests in the shape of Celine and John.

"I hope you don't mind, but when Joseph told us what had happened, we came straight over. We had our suspicions that you might be pregnant. Well, we hoped anyway."

"So, did I" I say crying again.

She just holds me and says, "It will be alright, you'll see. The pain won't last forever. Speaking as someone who knows."

"How many times did you go through this before you got your son?"

"Three or four," she says, "I lost count."

I just shake my head, unable to comprehend the enormity of it. I explain to her that Joseph has been shutting me out of late.

"Leave it to me. I hope you don't mind, but I have invited him over for dinner after work for a bit of mother and son time. I want to find out what is going on in that head of his before he bottles things up like last time."

"Good idea" I say gratefully. I cheer up a bit, spurred on by Celine and her wise words. Just then I hear his key in the door. His eyes look red and swollen but still incredible none the less.

It is good he is getting it out of his system.

"Sorry if you think I've been avoiding you, I just need time to get to grips with things. Get it all straight in my head. But I'm back now."

He walks over to me and sits down next to me. "We will have a baby of our own you know, just not yet."

I surprise him by saying, "I want to try again as soon as possible." I am worried if we don't it will never happen. It will become something we place in a box and turn the key on.

"What now?"

"Not now, I can't but soon. I just need to have one cycle according to the hospital. To check everything is back in working order."

"Let me know where and when and I'll be there."

"Glad to hear it. I can't start this one without you."

He laughs once again, revealing to me why I married him.

The next few weeks pass quickly, and I can feel myself getting irritable with people. What I am feeling is like PMT but this one is on steroids. I lose it with Hazel for no reason and then end up confessing everything to her over a cup of tea and a chocolate digestive which I dunked before placing in my mouth whole. She gives me a hug and tells me that she understands even though she hasn't been through it herself, she can appreciate the pressure I am under.

One of my other work colleagues has a wife that works at the same hospital as I had my operation. She was with me when I went down to theatre. Irritating as it was, I was glad to know I was in safe hands. But as a consequence of this, I am guessing a few people know now, anyway. Those that didn't, I tell eventually. It feels good to talk about it and get it out into the open. A way of getting free therapy, I guess. Hazel and I were becoming close. She was turning out to be a good friend despite our initial sparing contests. She is still very happy with Robert and they are even in discussions about buying a house together, which is great news.

My period comes and goes, and we prepare to launch ourselves into making the next version of Joe junior except this time one that is made of Teflon and can go the distance. Joseph goes out and purchases a Superman costume as a surprise for me. He is about to go through the rigmarole of putting it on when I tell him.

"Who needs Superman when I've got you?"

I take off his jacket and lead him by the tie to the bedroom, ready to show him my moves like Jagger. Technically, it should have been his tongue but who cares I think as I kick the bedroom door closed with my foot.

I wait for my next period to arrive, but it seems to have gone quiet on that front. I stop off and buy a couple of pregnancy tests on my way home the next day. All the while looking over my shoulder to make sure there is no-one, I know stood behind me in the queue. I decide to do it before he comes home from work. If it is negative, I will just not mention it. I leave the positive test proudly on the table next to the bed. He immediately notices it and say's

"Does this mean what I think it does?"

"Yes."

"That didn't take long." He says breathing on his fist and rubbing it on his chest.

"Alright, clever clogs. Just because you have Michael Phelps in sperm form, no need to blow your own trumpet."

"I wouldn't." he says immediately "Besides I have you to do that for me!"

"Don't be rude, the baby is listening."

"His ears are teeny tiny." he says laughing

"Not if he takes after his father."

"Okay, well I shall have to start calling you Noddy then and buy you a little red car to drive around in."

"I'm just winding you up. You're perfect. Besides you have the pen holder to prove it so it must be true."

Making it Happen

Over the next couple of months, I start to feel different somehow. I am beginning to get a nauseous feeling that comes and goes during the day, but it's nothing I can't handle. Joseph munches on protein bars while I gorge myself on folic acid. I am determined to keep my little rocky fighting fit. I have become repulsed by the smell of dishwasher tables which has worked in my favour as Joseph has had to take over those duties as well. Bit by bit I was getting myself excluded from everything domesticated, despite initially wanting to be a goddess in that department.

My sourdough intake has been limited as the smell of cooked breakfast has me running for the hills as well. My beloved tea has become like the devil itself, so I can't even enjoy the pleasure of that anymore. Instead, I am forced to drink hot chocolate vitamin drinks and large glasses of milk, but it would all be worth it in the end. That first cup of tea is going to be amazing, and I'm sure the baby won't be too bad either.

We have told a few people and they are cheering us on. The main ringleader being Abbey but closely followed by Celine and Hazel. Celine has gone knitting crazy I don't have the heart to tell her I am planning to kit the baby out in Ralph

Lauren, so I don't tell her and let her carry on regardless it seems less cruel somehow.

The love making has become a lot more sedate as we have swapped countertops in favour of a gentle roll on the bed minus the bouncing. Joseph thinks the philosophy of little and often should apply or big and often in his case. Poor Joe is probably sticking his fingers in his ears and shouting not again please make it stop.

We get the date for our twelve-week scan. Joseph seems to be under immense pressure at work and comes home in a horrible mood. I rush up and tell him excitedly about the scan, for him just to snap at me and tell me knowing our luck there will be something wrong again. I just walk away, unable to look at him anymore.

He runs after me and says "Sorry!" and begs me to forgive him.

I stroke his hair as a sign that I will, but I had been thinking exactly the same thing myself only yesterday.

The day before the scan, I am popping to the loo for the umpteenth time and notice blood. I panic and decide to phone Joseph at work, and I got to test my theory of how long it would take him to get home if he needed to. He is convinced it is because of what he had said and that he is somehow being punished for it. We make a silent trip to the doctors where I come face to face with Geena, the not so friendly midwife.

She spots Joseph and I see the penny drop as she realises why I let a large man like him impregnate me. She is confused as to why I am no further on with my pregnancy, so I explain what has happened. She seems to soften in light of this new information and takes my arm gently as she helps me climb on to the examination table.

"Let's have a look then," she says, pressing my tummy and using a machine to check the heartbeat.

Those few small minutes feel more like hours as I lie there with a traumatised Joseph stood beside me.

"Well, she says the heartbeat is strong, so I think everything is ok. Just come back if you are in any pain. Go to the scan as normal and they will check everything thoroughly while you are there. It is just something that happens sometimes, and it may happen every month throughout the rest of the pregnancy."

We attend our appointment and to our relief everything is fine. The only problem is that we don't get to find out the sex of the baby because they can't be completely sure, and they don't want to get it wrong. Joseph is frustrated by this and has a little sulk, but I don't care if it's Arthur or Mathur as long as the baby sticks around.

Joseph says, "You're right, a girl would be fine. We know two little girls that would be over the moon to have a third member of the unicorn gang."

I smile and agree. I take the scan pictures to bed with me that evening and just marvel at what we have created. Born out of a love of chocolate and him. I wonder if Joe himself will turn out to be a chocoholic. If he isn't, I want a refund because he can't be mine.

These days Celine is to be found walking around with a fixed grin on her face like she is an inmate at the home of the bewildered. The prospect of being a grandmother, a joy that is evident all over her face. The two of us have little shopping trips just to look at baby things but never actually buying anything as I want to wait to find out the sex rather than having to buy white. I want to buy everything in shades of blue to match his blue eyes which is another inevitability.

Joseph is already researching to see if IWC can make a miniature watch exactly the same as his. I do hope not. The thought of the two of them gazing at watches and talking about Ferrari's is not a prospect I relish. I hope instead he will be creative just like me. I imagine him as a toddler abandoning colouring books in favour of colour charts from Farrow &

Ball. I will spend my time teaching him how to say Stifkey Blue or Pure White.

"I wonder if he will have your colour eyes or mine?" I ask Joseph that night.

"Mine definitely," he says, "after all blue is the best colour." I imagine what he would look like with a black ring around each one of his and laugh to my-self. When he asks me what I am laughing at?

"I'm happy that's all." I secretly hoped Joe would have his father's eye's, but I don't want to admit that to him. A mini version in looks and size. I'd never get to look in a mirror again as the two of them would fight to check themselves out. I would spend all my time looking as though someone had pulled me through a hedge backwards with no make-up and unflossed teeth.

The time for our twenty-week scan arrives, and we make our way to the hospital. The baby is checked out thoroughly and everything is perfect. The bleeding has subsided now, which is good news. Joseph puts on a happy face in preparation for the nurse to tell us the sex of the baby. As Joseph is given the news that it is a boy, I fear he will explode he is so happy, and we go out for lunch afterwards to celebrate. He is silent and just sits there smiling in a world all of his own.

A world just for them I will only get to visit on special occasions. We drive over to the shopping outlet I had visited to buy his bathrobe all those months ago. It seems strange to be back here with him and now his son.

I wonder if the woman in Ralph Lauren would be working today as I want to show off a little. So proud am I of my husband and son to be. She doesn't seem to be here, so I busy myself looking at baby clothes instead. I wander around sedately for a bit before, in a frenzied attack, clear them out of anything blue I can get my hands on. Joseph phones Celine on the way home to give her the news. She is completely cocker-hoop at the prospect of another little prince to spoil rotten. We are at the halfway stage of the pregnancy and at last; I feel I am in a good place. Thank goodness.

Every Friday afternoon I visit Geena, the midwife. She checks Joe's heartbeat to make sure everything is still Okay. Just a little thing she has agreed to do for me to get me through to the end. That is when I get my mother-son bonding time. After my check-up, I go along to my antenatal class, held in a room at the back of the surgery.

Today we are to be taking part in an exercise class. We all lie on mats on the floor and wait for the lady that is running it to show up. She is a rather large lady who lectures us on health and fitness how we might think school is out for summer, but we have to keep ourselves in good health and not over-eat.

The lady next to me says, "Pot Kettle and Black!"

I just nod in agreement. She gets down on to the floor and then has to just roll back and forth on the mat till she gathers enough momentum to propel herself back up again. After she has gone, we just collapse in a fit of giggles.

Despite her words of warning, I am now the size of an average detached house. I don't think the alure of me dressed in sexy underwear gives Joseph the thrill it used to. Although he is too polite to tell me that. I think I could sew all of my old sets together and it still wouldn't cover everything.

"He is certainly going to be a big boy," Joseph says laughing.

"Don't tell me" I say, "Just like his father."

"They did say at the scan that everything was impressive."

"I don't think that was what they said. They just said he wasn't bashful. I wonder where he gets that from?" I say as Joseph lies next to me on the bed with nothing on, just preening himself. Not that I minded too much. I just had to be content with looking at him these days I don't have enough energy for anything else.

I feel like a snowball that is rolling and gathering extra layers all the time. So much so that I have given up weighing myself as it appears to be out of my hands anyway, it seems. All I know is my stomach is getting closer and closer to the steering wheel of my car. It won't be long before I get wedged and a hunky fire fighter has to turn up and cut me out. That would be another costume to add to the collection. If all else fails, we could open a fancy-dress shop.

Joseph is less like Mr Matthews and more like Mr Ben these days. I now plod up and down stairs rather than run, and my sexy walk is a thing of the past. It has turned into a slow waddle. He stands behind me now, waiting to catch me in case I fall. I think he is secretly hoping he isn't crushed to death under the weight of all the sausage rolls I've eaten that day.

"It's not my fault your son is addicted to pastry. I am merely following orders."

We can no longer share a bath together as I create such a tidal wave when I jump in that he is frightened he will get washed away somewhere. The shower is proving difficult as well and we look like two people who are playing a game to keep an enormous balloon between them and picking the soap up is a complete nightmare, you've got next to no chance of that. But we aren't complaining, how could we? We both wanted this so much, and we were now in touching distance. I have a mere three weeks to go before I am giving up work. This will hopefully free up the time to eat as many sausage rolls and pasties as my stomach desires. I picture myself lolling about watching This Morning and Loose Women while he works his balls off at work. I am looking forward to it already.

It is the third week in October, and I am due on New Year's Eve. I couldn't quite get the Christmas Eve I had hoped for, but you never know when Joe could decide he has had enough and make an appearance. Joseph is working hard at work so that once December comes, he can work from home if necessary, and David is being very amiable and helping out as much as possible. I think Abbey is responsible for the change in him. They both seem to be getting quite broody, so I wouldn't be surprised if Joe has a little play mate soon. I think that it is more about the fact we are having a boy that has got them thinking. I imagine the things the two boys could get up together and wonder if I can persuade Robert and Hazel to have a baby.

At last, it is time for me to give up work. I relish at the prospect as I am really tired all the time now. I have handed in my notice and have been training my replacement. I will miss my job, but I have been assigned a much bigger one and I want to give it my full attention. Joseph is very happy with the prospect of having a wife and child to come home to at the end of the day. I'm sure Celine would help out if I ever changed my mind and decided to return to work, but I think she is looking forward to the company. We will have enjoyable day trips to look forward to just the three of us. Poor John will have to start fending for himself again instead of relying on the art of telepathy to do it all for him. I feel quite sad as I clear my desk and say goodbye to the life, I had known for the last ten years. I shed a few tears as I bid my colleague's farewell. I was about to embark on a new chapter, besides, I'm sure Hazel and Robert will come to visit once the baby is born.

Work has given me lots of vouchers to spend on baby things so I can have a fun time spending those over the coming weeks. Joseph arrives to take me home. He is not happy about me driving myself anymore so has taken up the position of chauffeur as well as everything else. But he never moans or complains.

He waits patiently for me to come out. He can see I am upset, so he puts his arms around me for a bit before gently walking me around the car and helping me in. That night we sit and watch a movie just like old times. We kiss and canoodle like we did when it was just the two of us. Life before Joe was just a distant memory. "I have missed this," I say to him "us."

"Yeah, me too." He says smiling at me.

"We need to make the most of it because once Joe arrives, no-one else will get a look in." I explain to him.

"In that case." He jumps up and runs up the stairs.

"You have a bath while I walk up the stairs. It may take some time," I tell him. By the time I get up there I am out of breath, so I pause for few moments and open the door to find him fast a-sleep, so I just sigh and get in bed. I guess it is the thought that counts.

My Ta-da Moment

Decenber soon arrives, taking us by surprise. Joseph is now officially working from home or 'shirking from home' as he likes to call it. On a typical day, we get up, have breakfast together, do our own thing then meet up again for lunch. I take him tea and biscuits in his study in between. We are quite enjoying this new way of life. Some days if I get bored. when I have finished laughing with Phil and Holly, I join him in his study and quietly look at magazines in a corner and just watch him work. He pulls faces at the phone while David bangs on about cost projections and pie charts. The only pies I am interested at the moment come from Anton's bakery.

It is now the second week in December and Joseph has been working from home for two weeks. I have my weekly appointment with the midwife today, and this time Joseph is coming along for a change. The midwife takes one look at me and says I think we need to get you into hospital soon. Everything is looking a bit swollen, which bothers me. I seem to be gradually filling up with fluid, especially in my feet and legs. I just put it down to not being as mobile now as I have given up work. I know the baby is quite large and you are only small, so I don't want you to go full term. She makes a phone-call and then calls us back into her patient room. I'd like you to go in on Monday. I know it's only a few days from now, but I want you in there as soon as possible. I think it is the safest option.

We spend the weekend getting everything ready. The nursery has been finished for a while now, but Joe will sleep in our room with us to begin with. My bag is all packed and ready to go. I have trouble sleeping Sunday evening and I can't wait for the baby to be born so I can stop worrying. He is moving around less and less now, which is causing me concern.

We arrive at the hospital and wait to be taken into an examination room. My regular midwife is on call somewhere else, so is unavailable. She has promised me that I am in good hands and not to worry about anything. A doctor arrives and gives me medication that will start the labour process. Nothing is really happening, so he returns to give me an internal examination. When men say that watching their wife giving birth is like watching their favourite pub burn down, I think that is what Joseph is worried might happen. The pub wasn't burning, but he wasn't taking any chances.

All he kept saying was, "Have you seen the size of his hands?"

"Yes, I am aware of how big they are," I say, sounding

irritated as the doctor carries out another internal examination.

I have a restless night as Joe is now mobile again and turning around inside me. He is now quite large, and I can see elbows and knees as he tries to settle. I think he must be getting ready for the final push.

In the morning we are taken to another room to have my waters broken. I lie on the bed while the midwife punctures my amniotic sac. There is so much water that it is cascading everywhere. We laugh nervously while the nurse runs around mopping everything up furiously with paper towels. She checks the heartbeat and looks concerned. Joseph is looking unhappy and tries to find out what is happening.

"I need to get someone to check this, I won't be a second." Another nurse rushes in and then more people arrive. Suddenly people are rushing around me all shouting out different things to each-other.

"They will be alright, won't they?" Joseph asks a passing doctor.

"We need to act quickly, or we could lose both of them," the doctor tells him. It is as if someone has turned down the volume and everything is in slow motion. We both swallow hard as he takes hold of my hand.

"He just smiles and says if you think you are getting away from me that easily you can forget it." He is making a joke of it, but I can see him physically shaking before me. I try to say something meaningful, but I can't find the words maybe we don't need any.

If I have to go now, at least him and his blue eyes are the last thing I see as I close mine for what could be the last time. It is exactly how I would have wanted it. Only a chocolate bar is missing from his hand as he waves goodbye. It will not be my gift from god that gets to make the decision but the guy who sent him to me. I just hope he is feeling generous.

When I open my eyes, he is standing there with Joe in his arms. I have been asleep for a whole day, so I haven't seen much of Joe yet. But I have been assured he is feeding well.

"There's Mummy." Joseph says smiling at me. He picks up Joe's hand and pretends to wave. Joseph is holding a protein bar like a bottle in his other hand. "You haven't given him any of that, have you?"

No, besides, he is still full up from the Big Mac I gave him earlier.

"Hilarious,"

"Bring him here I want to see how handsome he is."

"What about me?"

"I know how handsome you are." I say smiling.

He is the picture of happiness as he walks around the bed proudly holding his son. My two favourite boys with me at last. I kiss Joseph and then Joe, who is peacefully sleeping. I get up and tip toe around getting my things together to leave the hospital. Just then Joe lets out a little cry and opens his eyes. I stare at him and see the familiar midnight blue that I have gazed upon a million times before. I wouldn't have had it any other way.

Now I have two twinkly skies to gaze upon.

"Ready?" he says, staring at me and holding out his hand.

"Ready. I was born ready!"

THE END – FOR NOW!

Acknowledgements

I would like to thank everyone that has inspired me to write this book. My husband and two sons, one of whom the character Joe junior is based upon.

I would like to thank all of my famous muses who all get a mention somewhere in the book. One of whom said recently after releasing his own book 'If not now, when?' and that, it appears, was all the encouragement I needed.

Cover illustrations from Katerina Izotova Art Lab

Printed in Great Britain
by Amazon